W9-BXX-084

DISCARDED NOV 0 6 2006

MAIN

Henry Potty and the Pet Rock

An Unauthorized Harry Potter Parody

VALERIE ESTELLE FRANKEL

COPYRIGHT

Printed in the United States of America

Published by WingSpan Press, Livermore, CA
www.wingspanpress.com

The WingSpan name, logo and colophon are the trademarks of WingSpan Publishing.

EAN 978-1-59594-088-9
ISBN 1-59594-088-x

First Edition 2006

Library of Congress Control Number 2006931446

To all those in need of healing through the joy of laughter.
I sure hope it helps.

Table of Contents

Introduction:
That Little Chapter Before the Prologue

Author's Note: The characters in this story are trained professionals. They have a great deal of experience at flying on vacuum cleaners, creating hot dogs by magical means, or scheming to achieve eternal life and total world domination. Please, do not try these things at home.

Supplementary Note: Adults, don't worry. This book is rated G and perfectly suitable for children of all ages. Children, don't worry. If your parents try to sneak the book away so that they can read it themselves, you can always hide it under the floorboards of a haunted, abandoned mansion with rhinoceros guards in pink polka-dot bathing suits to prevent anyone from taking it. Or failing that, it's small enough to go under your pillow.

Supplementary Supplement: This book has been translated from American English into British English. From there it was translated into English English, and then went through a brief stint in Swedish, just for a change of pace. After that it was translated back into American English with possible lapses, and currently exists as the original draft that you hold in your hands.

Supplement to the Supplementary Supplement: This is a work of fiction. However, all characters are probably disturbingly similar to characters you've seen in other places. Try not to be alarmed. After all, even serious characters need a vacation.

PS: Let's get on with the story already, shall we?

Prologue:
That Little Chapter After the Introduction but Before the Beginning of the Story

The world is full of miracles. When you buy a cinema hot dog and it's actually flexible, that is a miracle. When you tell the telemarketer that you're not interested, and he says, oh, ok, sorry to bother you, that's a miracle. When you get a letter in the mailbox saying you may have won a new car, that's just junk mail, we don't care about that right now.

On the steps of number 23232323.32 Privy drive, Somewhere in England, (land of Shakespeare, British accents, and saying crisps when you mean chips) a baby left in an asparagus crate on a doorstep screamed and screamed. His survival was another such miracle, given how many people wanted him dead. Or at least severely hurt. The asparagus seller probably would have settled for getting his crate back, since all of his little asparaguses were currently rolling about helplessly on the floor. But the incredibly evil bad guy planning to take over the world definitely wanted him dead. It was in his job description.

And so, this miracle baby lay in his asparagus box, wailing at an unjust world that really didn't care all that much. His speech, composed of such eloquent words as "Waaaaaaaaaaaaaaaah!" meant, in baby talk, "What do you mean I have to wait ten years before I'm the star of this book? I'm here, the readers are reading! I want fame, I want fortune, I want to see my lawyer, I want my own brand of breakfast cereal, I want..."

Fortunately for everyone concerned, ten years flew by in the space of a few lines, as the book propelled forwards to chapter one. Since he was the hero of the novel, the author couldn't drop an anvil on the whiny brat, much as she wanted to.

Chapter 1:

A PILE OF LETTERS

In a house so ordinary that it fairly screamed not to be noticed, from the beige carpet that went with everything (including stains) to the Beware of Rabid Hamster sign that kept out the salesmen, there lived a family. It was a perfectly ordinary family, consisting of Mr. and Mrs. Dorky, their son, Dumpy, and their gallant yet ill-treated household slave.

Oh, Henry Potty preferred calling himself a freedom-inhibited individual, but the name didn't change the situation as much as he'd hoped. Even subscribing to Menial Drudges United Newsletter did little to relieve his suffering. Still, Henry smiled through the abuse as Dumpy Dorky tried to pull his ears off and experimented on Henry with his sinister mold growing kit. For Henry knew that he was special. You see, he had…a destiny.

Henry had known this ever since he stumbled across the note that had been left beside his basket. All of the best heroes have been abandoned in baskets, starting with Breadbasket Fred, who went on to start a national chain of French fry restaurants. In any case, the letter caught Henry's attention thanks to the six inch letters on top that said, "Never, under any circumstances allow Henry Potty to read this letter." His cousin had left it in Henry's room, less from a sense of destiny and more from the fact that he still hadn't learned to read. He was only twelve, after all.

The letter read, "Destiny has marked this boy for greatness. Bring him up so he doesn't get a stuffed head. Oh, and make sure he wears clean socks. I can't abide foot fungus. Signed, a Mysterious Elusive Benefactor who prefers to remain incognito for the time being."

Henry knew that someday, someone would come and rescue him from his life of servile drudgery. Oh, not his parents. Lames and Jelly had been killed years ago, either from slipping on a pair of banana peels and falling to their deaths or getting hit by a rampant llama, his aunt didn't remember which. But someone, somewhere, cared enough to rescue him from a tragic life of foot fungus. And they would find him, eventually. Maybe. Henry was just glad he had so many definite facts to reassure himself with.

In the meantime, there was his fan club. Since Henry had a destiny, he knew that in the future, people would break down the doors of his house to beg for his autograph. Just as well to build his fan base now, so it would be all ready when fame and fortune followed. Besides, it gave him something pleasant to think about after his monthly scrubbing of his cousin's undershorts.

The letter came in a plain, ordinary, unassuming envelope, which Henry tossed under his bed carelessly. Probably another advertisement, or something equally not worth opening. His room was filled with "Henry Potty" books, card games, action figures, toothpick holders, movie posters and other rubbish. In short, everything that he needed to be a star. But whether his adventure appeared in the form of a gallant knight on a white horse or a mysterious lamp that would grant wishes and even polish his shoes, Henry knew it wouldn't be coming in an envelope. He began to update his website with a brand new, hot pink counter, (00000000000000000000000000000001 visitors have visited The Official Henry Potty Web Page) ignoring the fact that all the readers were smirking at his blissful ignorance.

The next day, there were two letters on his plate. Henry glanced at them briefly before going upstairs to alphabetize his chapter rules and bylaws for the Henry Potty Fan Club. An hour later, he was back downstairs, responding to his aunt's demands by painting tasteful murals on the disposal pipes under the sink. "Someday my fans will come," he sang, to the accompaniment of colorfully dressed singing mice. Twinkling, magical lights bounced from the pipes to his glasses, threatening to permanently fry his already pitiful vision. And so went the first week of mysterious mail.

☆ ☆ ☆

Henry's head jolted up as an earthquake shook the ground beneath him. A hideous, jello-like creature slithered down the stairs, all pale, lumpy, and alien. It was Dumpy Dorky.

Henry's cousin relied on the latest trends in skateboards since he was too fat to walk. And with his limited brainpower, he didn't have much of a glamorous future ahead of him. Perhaps he could make it as a disc jockey someday. Henry scrutinized his cousin again. Dumpy looked surprisingly happy for someone with that face.

"Henry, fetch me my slippers!"

Henry tossed them at his head. Luckily, Dumpy had moved onto another thought (he could only handle one at a time, on a really good day at least) and didn't notice.

"You know what I don't understand?" he said.

"Second grade geography?"

"No! Well, yes, that, but also why you get to be the star of the book. Shouldn't they pick someone with charm and style?"

"Like?"

"Me."

"You? You're less attractive than leftover gruel at Thanksgiving."

"Oh, that reminds me. I want a snack," Dumpy said. "It's been five minutes since I had breakfast."

"Of course, my little love-pudding," Piluffa said. Henry knew she called him that for his shape rather than his sweetness. Piluffa's long, pointy nose would've marked her as the evil stepmother type of woman, even if her stringy hair and green skin hadn't given her away. Henry's nicknaming her Aunt Pill completed the image. "Why don't I order the slave...er, your cousin, to fix you a nice cup of lard with a plate of double-stuffed cream buns and you can show me all the Q minuses on your report card."

Henry shuddered. Bread and water weren't so bad, considering. At least he knew that the source of Dumpy's quarrelsome mood was his being woken up really *really* early in the morning. It had barely been eleven AM when Henry had "accidentally" dropped the cast iron stove on the floor.

"Oh, Henry, I expect Dumpy wants some candy bars too," said Aunt Pilluffa.

Henry struggled to do the two chores at once, yet found it impossible. The candy bars were in the kitchen, while the lard was in the pantry and Henry just couldn't see a way to be in two places at once. At least, not and still be breathing.

"And I know you're occupied with shampooing the hamster and giving us pedicures and so forth, but take a moment to throw all these letters away. All two hundred-fifty-six of them clutter up the place and I can never have anyone to tea."

Pilluffa never had anyone to tea anyway, since even her dearest friends knew that she was the villainess of the book and refused to associate with her. Still, she could hope. Pilluffa plunged her sharp, evil stepmotherish fingernails in a bit deeper. "It could be fan letters."

"I doubt it," Henry sighed. "There isn't even a hint of a breeze coming out of them." Still, he picked up the top letter from the pile. At least someone out there wanted to hear from him. If he wrote back, at least he could include his recently updated Henry Potty Newsletter.

He opened the letter.

Dear Henry,

You probably haven't figured this out, but your frequent use of magic identifies you as a gizzard! If you are half as talented as you say you are, we would be happy to welcome you to our school. While you are researching the doubtless equally exemplary schools in England, you may want to consider sunny California for your student needs. Our school of Chickenfeet Academy looms over a beautiful, trash free beach, only minutes from the nearest strip malls, fast food joints, and of course, Hollywood. Some slanderous citizens have named us a fourth-rate school. This is entirely untrue! In fact, we feel proud to rank ourselves among the grandest third-rate schools of the nation. Word of your fame has reached us, even halfway across the world. Well, perhaps a third across the world. The Atlantic is a small ocean, as oceans go. Unless you compute by time zones, in which case it's the same as Hong Kong, just

in the opposite direction…where was I? Oh yes. Please
let us know if you're interested in being our first student
ever to graduate.

Yours truly,
Professor Bumbling Bore

"It sounds interesting," Henry said.
"You'd be gone all year?" his aunt wondered.
"Yep."
"Hmm, this sounds like a good program."

Menial Drudges United had been campaigning for years and were
slowly accumulating rights. In a few years they might even rebel
against mucking out stables. In the meantime, they were demanding
shovels.

So much authority in the hands (or rather, shovels) of slaves was
quite frightening for the innocent, hard working common folk who
had throttled them all those years. So now that the opportunity had
come to be rid of their household laborer, Henry's family jumped at
the chance. Well, his aunt and uncle jumped. Dumpy Dorky needed
several schoolmates heaving his excess flab before he could so much
as stand.

Within the week, Henry's bags were packed and he was ready to
go. His relatives herded him to the plane. "But I've never left England
before!"

"Shut up, we're giving you your freedom."
"Yes, those Americans will bring you up right."

His aunt and uncle bid him an emotional goodbye, even refraining
from throwing garbage at him. Dumpy showed no such restraint.

His fairy godmother was there to meet him when he got off the
plane. "Hello, my dear, I'm your fairy godmother. And I shall give
you a gown and a magic pumpkin coach, and everything that you
need to go to the ball!" She wore a fluffy pink taffeta gown, and
rosy high heeled shoes that raised her heels so far off the ground that
Henry was amazed she could walk. Henry noticed that the woman
was surrounded by singing birds, mice, and four off-key hedgehogs.

"I have a fairy godmother?"

"Everyone needs a godmother or godfather. Get serious!"

"Well, thank you for your offer, but I'm not going to a ball. I'm going to Chickenfeet Academy."

"Oh!" The woman flicked her wand, changing into pink army camouflage with tall, rosy combat boots. "Then let's hit those back to school sales!"

"Aw, why do I have to go shopping?"

"It's to bore the readers, so they'll be more impressed when something actually happens later in the book," his fairy godmother said.

"Why don't we just skip that section?"

Henry left the store carrying all the things that he would need in the following year, including a cauldron, as well as a hot-drun, several gizzard bathrobes in a variety of tasteful colors with color-matched socks and hair ribbons, a small set of scales, the snake that the scales came off of, several grapefruit, and a small elephant.

"Wait, you forgot your wand!" his godmother protested, scurrying to catch up after all the pages her fairy godson had skipped.

Henry left the store carrying all the things that he would need in the following year, including a cauldron, a hot-drun, several gizzard bathrobes in a variety of tasteful colors with color-matched socks and hair ribbons, a small set of scales, the snake that the scales came off of, several grapefruit, a small elephant, and a magic wand.

"Not like that," his godmother scolded. "The wand, at least, you're buying properly."

She led him to *The Wand Guys*, and pushed him inside. "Henry Potty," murmured a tall, attractive woman with rosy cheeks and an umbrella. She held a tape measure up to his ear and let the other end fall to the floor. "Not an ideal charge for nannies. Doesn't put his socks away."

"Aren't you in the wrong book, dear?" Henry's godmother asked.

"You haven't advertised for a nanny?"

"Dear me, no! Henry's going off to Chickenfeet Academy."

"I'm sorry to have troubled you, then."

"Oh, no, not at all. I have to go meet Sleeping Beauty in a few pages anyway," the godmother said.

The mysterious nanny raised her umbrella and flew off with it, soaring higher and higher into the sky. After a few moments came a screech of dismay and the twang of overstretched telephone wires. Henry's fairy godmother turned her attention to Henry, who was busy counting the dots in the ceiling and trying to find patterns in them, despite the fact that the ceiling was solid black.

"Henry! Wake up. You need to get a wand."

"Really? Most people say I need to get a life. I suppose a wand would be easier."

Henry's godmother sighed. "All right. Now, stand on one foot, put the other leg behind your head, and hold your arms out in front of you. Then shut your eyes. Oh, and try to wiggle your ears."

Henry did as he was told. "So this will help you figure out what kind of wand to get me?" He heard a faint humming sound. Perhaps it was a burst of magic delving into his soul to find him the perfect wand to treasure for the rest of his life.

Actually, it was the record button on his fairy godmother's video camera. "No, this is for my submission to America's Funniest Fairygodchildren," she said.

"But what about my wand?" Henry asked, still trying to wiggle his ears.

"Oh. Here." She pulled the closest wand off a shelf and tossed it to Henry, who jumped and caught it in his mouth while still maintaining his awkward position. "Good boy!" his godmother said. "Goodness, I could make twice as much money if I submitted this to America's Funniest Pets as well. Here, have a treat!" She tossed him a piece of candy and he opened his mouth wide to catch it, letting the wand drop in the process. The wand landed on his one supporting foot and he hopped about in pain, the chocolate bar still clenched in his teeth.

His godmother kept the camera rolling. "Gee, this'll make me a million. Maybe I could even go on that island show and make some real money."

Finally, Henry realized that he had his wand now, and didn't need to keep hopping with his other leg squashed behind his head just to entertain his fairy godmother and millions of Americans with nothing better to watch on TV. So he stopped.

Henry's fairy godmother sighed in disappointment and turned her camera off. "Guess there's nothing more to see." Bigfoot flew by the store window, riding on a UFO, but neither of the humans noticed. "Well, be good, Henry, and have fun in school," his godmother said.

"Wait! Don't I get wishes or blessings or anything?"

"Hmm, that's a good idea. At least it might keep you out of trouble." The fairy bopped Henry on the head with her wand.

"What did you do?" he asked.

"I hit you on the head with my wand. My goodness, couldn't you tell?"

"No, I mean, what did it accomplish?"

"It was fun." She bopped him a second time. "And that one's to bang some sense out of you." Immediately a small trickle of pennies cascaded from Henry's ears as Henry groaned. Being hit with a wand was bearable, but his godmother's pun was not.

"All right, fine, I'll give you your present." She waved her wand in an arc over Henry's head. Immediately, a brilliant light flooded down from above, blinding Henry and forcing him to squint.

"Could you turn that down?" he asked.

"Certainly." The light swiveled downwards to glare even closer to Henry's watering eyes.

"No, I mean turn down the intensity." Immediately, the brightest part of the light shot even closer to Henry and he covered his eyes in desperation. "Turn it off!" he howled.

"Of course, of course, no need to holler. Well, at least you seem a little brighter now. If we keep this up, you might even pass a few of your classes." The light thankfully dimmed.

"But what does the light do?" Henry asked.

"It's your conscience, Henry. When it glows like that, it means you've done a good deed. I just wish crickets weren't becoming an endangered species. This will send my electricity bill through the roof. Well? Aren't you going to say thank you?"

Henry grimaced. He wasn't that grateful for an enormous spotlight, and a conscience interested him even less. "Fairy Godmother? I was hoping for something a bit more substantial." Henry rubbed his fingers together in the universal sign for money.

His fairy godmother reached into her pink purse and retrieved a lint-covered lollipop. "Everything all right now? Good," she said and she vanished, not before smearing his forehead with a big, moist kiss, nearly taking the skin off in its intensity.

Then she popped back in. "Nearly forgot! Just remember, always let your conscience be your guide. Oh, and wear clean underwear." Then she popped out, leaving an aroma of lavender laundry soap and the bright tinkle of artificial music lingering in the air.

"Right," Henry said. "Conscience, how do I get to the train station?"

Blazing gold letters appeared in the sky before him. "What do I look like, the yellow pages? I'm only around to pick on you when you screw up, and heap guilt onto already bad situations. Now go call information and find someone who cares. And get a haircut."

"What good will cutting one of my hairs do?"

A large number of golden asterisks, exclamation points, and so forth implied that his conscience was busy spewing dirty words. "And another thing," the letters added. "It's not the Chickenfeet train, it's the Chickenfeet trainer."

Two exhausting hours of scurrying and begging for directions from anyone who looked remotely gizzardly later, Henry found himself at the trainer station. Asking for directions hadn't been so terribly embarrassing; he had just asked the wrong people. Gizzards could easily be identified under normal circumstances, since they were the ones wearing bathrobes and dunce caps. However, today was the insane asylum's monthly trip to the zoo, and they were all taking the train.

After Henry asked the fifth straitjacketed individual if he knew where Henry could take a giant sneaker to get to a castle called Chickenfeet that was full of gizzards, the white-clad attendants began to watch him with more than polite interest. After two of them started measuring him for his straightjacket size, Henry decided it would be a good idea to sprint in the opposite direction. Unfortunately, he became tangled with a rather large marching band that was going in the completely wrong direction, and after seeing his magic wand, all seventy-six trombone players decided he must be their conductor. Weary and bruised from being jabbed by all the trombones as the metal pieces (which are actually called slides, aren't you glad you learned something today?) had banged into him, Henry finally arrived at the Chickenfeet trainer.

It was a giant tennis shoe, in day-glow orange fierce enough to

9

blind a bat. The Chickenfeet Trainer stood several stories high, with purple laces and puffy glitter stickers all over it in a rainbow of colors. The effect was rather like popping one's eyes into a blender, putting it on extra-high, and then reaching in between the still-twirling blades to pop the eyeballs back into one's head. (Please don't try this. It's very bad for the blenders. In fact, the blender companies have already written forty-three letters of complaint. Be nice to blenders. Blenders are our friends.)

Henry hurried up to the old woman who stood beside the trainer taking tickets. "Are you the conductor?"

"No, young man. I'm just the old woman who lives in this shoe. I don't know what I'm going to do with all you children. Do you have a ticket?

"Yeah, I guess." Henry vaguely remembered his fairy godmother giving him a ticket. Unfortunately, it was nowhere in sight. "Would you take this instead?" Henry asked, offering the lint-covered lollipop. But the woman was no longer paying attention to Henry's words. Instead, she stared at his forehead, her eyes widening until they were big as spotlights. "What's *that* on your forehead?"

"Huh?"

"That's a magic birthmark, isn't it?"

"I have a birthmark?"

"Go on board, please. Don't let me stop you, oh no. More than my life is worth to stop someone with an unsightly mark bestowed on him by destiny."

A bit puzzled at the obsequious shoe owner, Henry hurried on board, taking a moment to glance in the mirror in the train's bathroom. Gobs of bright red lipstick plastered his forehead in a wiggly horizontal shape, rather like a snake trying to tap dance.

After spending hours trying to chip, scrape, and scrub the red goo from his face, Henry returned to his seat. Time to brighten up his trip by indulging in some overpriced goodies. At the exact moment he thought that, the candy cart coincidentally rolled around, pushed by a witch in a purple-spotted bathrobe with a little white apron on top.

"Whatcha want?" she asked, chomping on her gum like a waitress in a truck stop.

"What've you got?" Henry asked.

"Let's see, Sarm bars, Sernicks, Popsie roll toots, polilops, and tot parps.

"Those names sound awfully familiar," Henry said, staring at the colorful wrappings as he tried to discern what they contained. The cart displayed all sorts of other fascinating things as well. Spinach and jellybean sandwiches, prune nuggets, beef 'n' cheese ice cream, and plenty of other snacks that Henry couldn't envision eating, even if he were starving. The insoles of his tennis shoes looked far more palatable.

"Oh, yeah, they are. We just scrambled the names of the candies to make them sound more original."

"Well, I don't know…"

"Would you prefer many-flavored bugs or chocolate hogs? We got those, too."

"Er, that's all right. I think I'll try the MM&s. I have no idea what that name unscrambles to."

The candy cart witch rolled her eyes as she served Henry his snack. "Looks like you'll fit right in with the rest of the new students."

Chapter 2:

OF RATS AND GIZZARDS

Waiting on the Chickenfeet platform to greet them was Higgle. He was large and rather hairy. Completely hairy, in fact. Brownish fur that smelled suspiciously of gumdrops and sarm bars ballooned out from him in a perfect sphere, concealing everything but his face and the giant white tennis shoes that stuck out the bottom. He had round, googly eyes that jiggled as he leaped back to avoid being trampled as the Chickenfeet Trainer came to a halt. And finally, Higgle wore a giant set of TV antennae so that he'd be sure to be spotted and recognized. Besides, they were wonderful for lulling his pet rabbit, The Destroyer, into a state of calm. In short, Higgle looked like a giant fuzzy weeple.

Chickenfeet Academy towered above the students. Well, actually, it would be more accurate to say that the Academy bounced, jiggled, and more or less threatened to tumble down on their heads. The Chicken Feet themselves stretched hundreds of feet into the sky, as they pranced about in front of the trembling students. The Chicken Feet kicked, minced, tiptoed, and even got in a bit of Irish step dance before a bathrobed teacher ordered them to stop. The castle sat above them, bouncing in the wind as the Chicken Feet cavorted. Henry swallowed hard. He could already feel his stomach revolting at the thought of living in such a seasick, jolting place. Besides, from the smell of them, the feet hadn't been washed in quite a long while.

"Fherfunger legcrakl" said Higgle.

"What?" asked a number of the students as they stood there in multicolored bathrobes. Several of them had already formed the instant friendships that would last for a lifetime. Others just wanted their mommies to come rescue them from the weird gizzards.

"He said, 'New students this way,'" said the resident ghost who had the assignment of following Higgle around and translating his incomprehensible accent for the benefit of the incoming students.

They all paraded into Chickenfeet. Standing in the doorway to greet them was Bumbling Bore, the principal of the school. He wore hot pink surfer shorts, a t-shirt that was daringly cut to reveal his lack of muscles, and a pair of sunglasses with little palm trees on the sides. His glaring green button said, "Just 6 years, 3 months, and 202 days left till retirement." The principal's long, white beard trailed on the ground, collecting candy wrappers and dog droppings.

"That's Bumbling Bore," Henry heard someone whisper. "The only gizzard Lord Revolting fears." An ominous rumble of thunder rumbled ominously somewhere off in the distance.

"Why's that?" someone asked.

"He has Lord Revolting's credit card numbers." The thunder rumbled again, this time sounding more like the ca-ching of a cash register.

"Why do you say gizzard?" Henry asked. Had he come to the wrong school? Could he get a refund?

"It's a new age, California thing." The speaker smoothed back his spiky purple hair to reveal eight earrings per ear with hands displaying fourteen different shades of nail polish. His robe was tie-dyed in a rainbow of colors. "I should know; I'm from around here."

"Oh, all right, then."

"You know, there's lots of other cool California stuff," the colorful student said, determined to welcome the English visitor with proper courtesy. His friends smirked.

"You're not going to tape a Kick Me sign to my back, are you?" Henry asked. "We have that one in England, too."

"What? Oh, of course not. But walking around with a sign saying, 'Laugh At Me, I'm From Far Away' will make everyone accept you."

"And ask people for swirlies," a tiny girl with two brown braids added. "You'll love swirlies."

"Or, or hunting fried chickens," another boy added. "They live around here, see, and you just have to hold a bag open and call—"

"Welcome to Chickenfeet," Bumbling Bore interrupted from his podium. "All of you new students have an exciting year in store for you, filled with—" Here he was interrupted by loud snores as the entire school's new class tumbled to the ground fast asleep. To put it simply, Bumbling Bore was duller than an in flight magazine on *Air Sweden*.

When Bumbling Bore had finished his speech, being careful to start over from the very beginning whenever an untimely snore interrupted him, dinner was long over. In the interests of having the students awake enough to be assigned to dorms, he let another teacher take over the rest of orientation.

"We do dorm selection here by a totally fair and arbitrary process," said Millie McGonk, as the students piled into the Sort-of Room. Millie McGonk was tall and stately, with a long nose and four green eyes (she wore spectacles). She also had blue fur, owing to a magical experiment a few years before when she tried to turn herself into a cat and ended up as a blue, fuzzy monster with googly eyes and an insatiable hunger for cookies. Newly obsessed with cookies in every size, shape, and color, Miss McGonk let her magical studies slide and only continued teaching at the request of Bumbling Bore, who thought it made his school seem more equal opportunity, as it proved that he would hire people no matter what their color, or length of fur.

"We have four fine dormitories here," Miss McGonk said. "The Heroes' Dorm, The Dummies' Dorm, The Scumballs' Dorm, and the Leftovers' Dorm. Each of these housing facilities waits eagerly to welcome you. Very soon, our volunteers will bring in the Sorting Rat. Just hold out your finger and let the rat bite it. In that moment, before all the pain sets in, you'll hear a voice in your head and know which dorm you should be in. Then we'll start our tour of campus, beginning with the cookie shelf in the kitchen and continuing on to the infirmary and the band-aid cabinet. Also, I'd like to introduce Mr. Filth. He's our resident spy and tattletale. If he sees anyone doing anything he's suspicious of, it's his job to alert the authorities."

"And I will," Filth promised. "Alert is my middle name." He was a three foot tall, rat-faced man, wearing a trench coat, deerstalker hat, bandolier full of variously sized magnifying glasses, and Agatha Christie style high heels. Tucked under his arm was his Crime Fighting kit: a butterfly net, police whistle, a fake mustache for disguises and a stack of Solve-it-Yourself mysteries (recommended for ages 6-8).

Miss McGonk motioned to two students in the corner. Both of them pulled on heavy gloves that were covered in numerous scratches and bite marks. They left the room, and then returned a moment later, lugging between them a gray rat that must have weighed about fifty pounds. They set it reverentially on the floor, and then scurried away before it could bite them. The sharp-toothed, corpulent rat stood on the floor, belly dragging unsupported by the spindly legs. It gnashed its teeth and craned its neck for a victim.

"Don't crowd, everyone will have a turn," the teacher called. "Don't get too close to him or you'll make him nervous."

Henry watched as each student held out his or her finger to the rat, and then shrieked in agony as it bit. Each of them screamed out a dorm name, which Miss McGonk diligently wrote on her pad. Finally it was Henry's turn. "Um, thanks, but I've decided to go back to England. I won't be needing a dorm."

"Don't be ridiculous," the teacher said. "Your relatives sent a note saying that they never want to see you again for as long as you live, until summer. Then they'll welcome you with open arms and you can spend three months trying to catch up on a year's chores. Now hold out your finger."

Turning away and shuddering, Henry extended his finger towards the slobbering rat. He felt the jaws clamp down on his helpless digit, then spit it out with a choking sound. Just as Henry's eyes bugged out in agony, he heard a soft, whispering voice say, "Dummies' Dorm."

Okay, Henry thought. I may be in pain but I'm not stupid enough to spend all year in the Dummies' Dorm. "What was the first one again?" he asked Miss McGonk as she stood, clipboard waiting.

"The Heroes' Dorm."

"Yes, that's it, exactly. That's the one I'm in."

"Ah, good." The teacher made a small note on the clipboard. "Now let's go visit the infirmary. But first, I need cookies! Must have cookies!" Abandoning her dignified walk, she bolted for the kitchen as fast as she could run, with all of her students scurrying behind her.

☆ ☆ ☆

By the time they reached the Heroes' Dorm, Henry was fainting from hunger, thanks to missing dinner. Miss McGonk had eaten all the cookies, so he hadn't even had a snack. Luckily, his aunt and uncle had sent him a care package of instant gruel. The children walked up to the painting that hid the entrance to the dorm. A portrait of a lady, plump enough to spill out of her picture frame on all sides, blocked the passageway, stinking of mothballs. Henry stood in front of the picture and recited the password. "The fat lady sings."

"What? You think I'm fat! How dare you! And no, I certainly won't sing. Be gone, wretched boy."

Higgle mumbled to her for a few moments until finally the pacified Viking portrait allowed the children to enter.

Most of the students ended up in the Heroes' Dorm. According to Higgle, this generally happened, which was why they won the official Good Guy Award every single year. At least, that's what Henry thought he had said. As Henry settled in and unpacked his hundreds of fan posters, muscle tone calendars and autographed toilet tissue, two children his own age appeared at the door.

One had shocking red hair that probably saved him a great deal of expense on flashlight batteries. His vacant grin indicated that most of his contributions to group projects would be suggestions on breaking for lunch. He wore a purple sweater that said in big, hot pink letters "My mother couldn't afford to go somewhere exotic, so she just made me this dumb sweater by hand." A little label on the collar said "Loving Touches."

Something about the girl beside him indicated that she was, in fact, a girl. She seemed to have inherited her companion's intelligence as well as her own, judging by the ruler, protractor, calculator, compass, digital thermometer, and pair of extra socks protruding from her top right-hand pocket protector (all geniuses know how important extra socks are).

"Are you fans?" Henry asked. "You're a bit early; I mean, I won't be famous and popular until the book's end. But if you'd like to see the room where I actually stayed during my days here at Chickenfeet, I could—"

"Huh? We're your roommates," the boy said.

17

Henry felt his dreams of fame and adoring girls ripping his bathrobe to pieces for souvenirs vanishing away like the last little bit of lollipop when you've gotten tired of the whole stick thing and just bite the last bit of candy off in one big chomp. "Do you even know who I am?"

"Henry Potty, son of Lames and Jelly Potty," the girl said. "You're spending the year here in California because your relatives got tired of having you pick up after them. By doing every single bit of work until they could no longer manage for themselves, you were propelling them into an idyllic life where they would become overdependent on you and no longer even manage to tweeze their nose hairs unassisted. Either that or they know you're an arrogant little snot obsessed with your nonexistent fans and they wanted to dump you as soon as possible. You want to study transformation, conjuration, and recycling while you're here at the Academy. Oh, and you want to be discovered by Hollywood."

"How did you know all that?" Henry asked.

"My name's Horrendous Gangrene. I know everything."

"Besides, everyone knows you're on the gizzer-net," the boy added.

"How many fingers am I holding up behind my back?" Henry challenged Horrendous.

"Eight."

"That's amazing!" Henry said, failing to notice the mirror that hung on the wall behind him. "Just remember, the important thing is that I'm the legendary hero of the book."

"Hey, that's super, man," the boy said. Henry didn't bother asking his name, since he figured the readers already had a general idea who he was, even if the book called him "the boy."

"So the boys are gizzards here at Chickenfeet," Henry observed with his usual brilliance. "What are the girls called?"

"Well, for the majority of the time, I prefer to identify myself as a magically-enabled individual," Horrendous said.

"You're a which?"

"Exactly."

"Exactly what?"

"No, exactly which."

"Which what?" Henry felt his melted brains beginning to dribble out his ears.

"No, just which."

"Which?"

"Yes. You're finally getting it."

"I am? Getting what?"

"Not what. Which."

"Argh!!!"

After hours of circling about until Henry felt incredibly dizzy, he managed to conclude that Horrendous, along with all the other females at the school, were in fact whiches. Apparently, witches with traditional spelling were known for doing some nasty spelling indeed, such as constructing houses out of sweet-smelling gingerbread, then forcing greedy little potential thieves to keep eating until they were sick. New age whiches tried original and radical approaches, such as forcing people to attend self-empowerment seminars until their brains went numb, then feeding them mysterious vegan dinners. The Which Committee had just gotten around to updating all their stationery and memo pads, and even put out their first issue of Which's Which magazine. They'd beaten the where?-wolves by two weeks.

"So you're a gizzard, right?" Henry asked the boy, desperately hoping for a return to normalcy.

"Yes. I'm Really Wimpy."

"You shouldn't say things like that about yourself."

"Why not? That's my name, Really Wimpy." Apparently, he had just enough gumption to not wait any longer for the book to introduce him without his preempting the issue. "And this is my pet rock, Flaky," added the boy now known as Really Wimpy. Flaky was round, gray, good-sized, and to all appearances, a perfectly normal example of his species.

"What do you do with a pet rock?"

"Oh, we have wonderful conversations."

Henry decided not to comment. "Once I had a pet goldfish, but my parents' trusted friend, Lord Revolting, betrayed us and murderously flushed it down a toilet."

Horrendous gasped. "That's terrible!"

"You mustn't say that name!" Really Wimpy protested at the same time.

"Why?"

"It's a nickname he made up to scare people."

"Hush!" Horrendous said. "We're not supposed to find that out until book 2. No one knows what Lord Revolting's real name is."

"Why?" Henry asked.

"Because he won't tell us."

"Did he really murder your goldfish?" Really Wimpy asked.

Henry nodded. "But I'll always remember what he looked like, because he had three extra hairs in his right eyebrow. You don't forget a thing like that. One day I'll find him, and go up to him and say—"

"Hello, my name is Henry Potty, you killed my goldfish, prepare to die?" Horrendous guessed.

"Well, I was going to say, 'You're really mean!' But I guess your idea is good, too," Henry said gallantly. The blinding light from up above glowed briefly, as if knowing that he had only been good to impress his new friends.

Henry's acquaintances didn't offer to stay long, since they apparently had better things to do than admire Henry's collection of Henry Potty Original Kindergarten Clay Shapes. Horrendous mumbled, "I need to go wash my hair or my laundry; I forget which." Really Wimpy gazed after her with wide, tearful eyes, obviously wishing that he had thought of such an airtight excuse.

Ominous music burst ominously through the air as Lord Revolting strode ominously into the room, smelling like week-old catfish. He was tall, dark, and incredibly ugly, with green makeup slathered over his skin to increase his evil appearance. The Halloween costume that he wore had once been a wicked witch's dress, at least a wicked witch who was forty-seven and into her second husband and fifth pregnancy. Yards of extra black fabric hung off him like moldy curtains. All forms of trash coated the dress, from cream-filled cupcake wrappers to disposable diapers.

"Revolting!" Henry gasped, too startled to speak coherently, let alone come up with a witty and memorable speech that brain-cell-deprived fantasy fans could quote for decades afterwards, for lack of anything better to contribute to society.

"Don't say that name!" Really Wimpy shrieked.

Henry turned to see his new friend cowering in the corner. "Oh. Okay, I won't say it. What should I call him, then?"

"You know who."

"No, I don't know. That's why I asked."

"No, call him you know who."

"But what if he doesn't know? I mean, I don't want to spend hours explaining it all to him if he's too ignorant to grasp—"

"Excuse me," Lord Revolting interrupted. "But I came here to do some general terrifying and threatening, not to listen to you two babble. Do you realize I had to crawl up the fire escape, near those dumpsters in the alley? I fell four times. You certainly keep this place locked up. But I have triumphed, nonetheless!" He drew himself up proudly, and then realized he'd been caught in bad lighting. He swiftly moved two feet to the left, where a dramatic shaft of moonlight hit the floor, and resumed his haughty pose.

"Why have you come?" Henry asked.

"Why, to spoil the book for you, of course. That's the most evil thing that I could possibly do. I may as well tell you now that I'm the one behind all of the malevolent schemes in the book. I doubt you'd figure that one out, anyway. At the book's end I will appear and maliciously taunt you again. Not to mention trying to kill you. That said, enjoy your school year. Isappear-day!" And Lord Revolting disappeared.

"Phew, he's gone," Henry said.

A disembodied voice floated out of the air. "Not completely, Henry. I'll be watching you." A few final bars of creepy music sounded.

Really Wimpy shuddered. "He's worse than my mom!"

Henry wandered around his new school, taking time to find out where the closest hairdresser was to class and how to cheat the candy machines on each floor. Higgle was giving tours, but Henry didn't feel like translating his long speeches. Rumor had it that Bumbling Bore had once conducted all the tours, until parents complained about their children falling into the lake and drowning before they could wake up.

The Chickenfeet library was managed by an elderly goat whose most famous contribution to literature involved eating the world's largest collection of eighteenth century knitting almanacs. Not to mention all of the digests. After she polished off the school's card catalogue for dessert, a universal motion appointed her chief librarian. No one else had a clue how the books were sorted, without all the little cards to guide them. Now Gallicia goat grazed greedily on the glorious gorges of Great Books, grinning as only a grizzled goat could grin.

Henry walked into the library, hoping for something classical and inspiring with a maximum of one word per page. He headed for the picture book section, but was arrested by the sight of a gleaming book entitled *Defeating Lord Revolting for Lamebrains*. Just as he reached for it, he skidded to a sudden halt. "You!"

Lord Revolting jumped at Henry's dramatically vague exclamation, and dropped the book he'd been thumbing through. Henry frantically scanned the wall until he saw the expected square case. Its large letters read, "In case of evil gizzards, break glass." Henry picked up the tiny hammer beside the case and shattered the thin barrier between him and the object he sought.

It was a squirt gun, with icy water guaranteed to melt any which or gizzard into a bubbling puddle of green goo. Henry snatched the water pistol and took careful aim. "Fancy destroying the bad guy this early in the book," he thought to himself, with a well-deserved grin of triumph. Unfortunately, his smug thoughts took up just enough time for Lord Revolting to metamorphosize into a wooden bat, and smash his way out the window. Henry dropped the squirt gun on the floor, and did his best not to break into a long, loud tantrum. So close, yet not close enough.

Lord Revolting's book lay open on the floor on the other side of the room, face down. Henry hurried over to it. Printed in dripping red letters on the black cover were the words, *Truly Evil Spells for Idiots*. Henry picked it up, careful to hold the book open where Lord Revolting had been reading. Perhaps the evil gizzard's research would indicate what he was planning.

Henry stared at the page in question for a very long time. Then he actually read it. It said, "Spell to live forever and become the most powerful evil gizzard in existence." A faint stink of garbage rose from the pages. It smelled anything but roselike.

The page said:
(Well, actually, it didn't say anything; Henry had to read it.)

Spell to live forever and become the most powerful evil gizzard in existence:

In order to live forever and become the most powerful evil gizzard in existence, follow these steps.

Fill your veins with unicorn blood to cause yourself to live forever.

Mix the following in a bowl:

Two magical hot dogs
A used postage stamp
Toilet paper (pink, preferably unused)
One handful of magical mushrooms
The powdered remains of a runaway pet rock

Drink your newly created potion of evil power.

Warning: No refunds.

Henry dropped the book as if it had burned him. (Well, actually, it had. It doesn't pay to go around handling evil books, after all.) He had to tell his friends. Maybe together they could figure out what Lord Revolting planned to do.

After a long consultation with Horrendous Gangrene and Really Wimpy, the three children decided that they needed to stop Lord Revolting. After a few more hours of debate, they decided to look for the items that Revolting wanted, in order to keep him from getting them. Henry immediately voted to hide all the toilet paper in the school. "That way, Lord Revolting won't find any," he explained.

"Well, yes, but hiding all the toilet paper in Chickenfeet still might not be the best idea," Horrendous said. She didn't explain why, since she figured any child over the age of three could figure it out. Henry's blank stare indicated that he didn't have a clue. Horrendous didn't bother filling him in. "Maybe you should just stand wherever there's pink toilet paper and yell for help if Lord Revolting tries to enter the room."

The boy's bathroom was all out of pink toilet paper, so Henry stationed himself directly outside the girl's bathroom, ignoring the girls' insults and pummeling as they entered. Apparently they thought he was rather odd for standing there. Then someone in a long, black bathrobe hurried past, sticking foully of garbage.

Henry wanted to follow him in, but the terrifying smells of perfume and hairspray stopped him before he could open the door. So he resolved to wait and catch the person when he left. If it was Revolting, he would make him relinquish any pink toilet paper he had with him.

Henry waited a few minutes, then a few more. At last, half an hour had passed. How long could Lord Revolting take? Just because he was a thoroughly evil villain who could flush goldfish without a second thought shouldn't mean that he didn't use the bathroom like any normal person.

"Aha!" Henry jumped ten feet into the air as Mr. Filth tackled him from behind with the aid of a stepladder. "Get to class," the sneaky little man snarled silkily. "You shouldn't be here, not unless you've had a gender-change operation and you're now Harriet Potty. Remember, I always enforce the rules. Law enforcement is my middle name."

Henry shamefacedly left the area, falling into step with a short little girl just leaving the bathroom. She had two brown pigtails, thirty-seven red freckles, and one round nose that seemed to take up half her face. Her black gizzard bathrobe appeared far too big for her, and she stumbled as she walked up the hall beside him.

"Who're you?" he asked.

"I'm Miffie. Miffie Muffet. Everyone around here learns to respect me very quickly."

Henry had to smile. "You sure are little, Miffie Muffet. You don't look that intimidating to me."

"Some call me Miffie the Terrible."

"And what do the rest call you?" Henry asked.

"M&M," Miffie muttered.

"Okay, now I'm really curious. Why would anyone call you Miffie the Terrible?"

24

"I beat up wimpy little first years like you."
Henry burst into laughter.

A few minutes later, Henry trudged over to the infirmary.
"Hell-o," a bubbly, blonde nurse chirped. "What seems to be the trouble?"
"What do you thingk?" Henry asked in a stuffy, barely recognizable voice. "I have a wangd up by ngose."

Chapter 3:

A REAL LADIES MAN

The nurse pondered Henry's situation for a long minute. "Yes, it appears you do. Let me call the doctor in."

The doctor arrived speedily and proceeded through a careful inspection of Henry's nose. "Yes, I think you do have a wand there. I'll have to run some tests to be certain, you understand, but my preliminary prognosis is that you have, in fact—"

"Rebove it!" Henry demanded.

Outside, a few minutes later, Higgle straightened in surprise as a wand shot out the window as if fired from a bow and shot him in the furry head.

Higgle shook his head. Nothing important had been hit, at least. He picked up the wand and mumbled something vaguely similar to, "A wand. Hot dog!"

A jumbo hot dog promptly appeared on the lawn. Laughing like a child with a new toy, Higgle picked up both wand and hot dog, and resumed his walk towards the library to find an English-Mumble/Mumble-English dictionary.

Inside, Henry lay back on a bed recovering from the eeze-snay ort-snay spell. A vase of dead lilies sat on the bedside table. The bed itself was adjustable, able to turn over up to 360 degrees and dump its occupant neatly on the floor. Henry had tested it fully eight times before figuring out exactly what it did. The ceiling was a beige so innocuously monotonous that Henry felt his eyes filming over just looking at it. His conscience swiveled around the room, as if uncertain whether to praise him for not hitting back or discipline him for shrieking in terror and running from a girl a foot shorter than he was. On his panicked run, he had dashed through the girls' locker room, resulting in slaps, screams, and several beatings from a barbed towel.

Henry switched on the TV, flipping between the two static-filled channels. He could choose between turn of the century *Lassie Meets Flipper* reruns and the home shopping show in Japanese. He pressed the red button beside the bed. The nurse came in, glancing over a pile of forms as she did so. Her platinum-blonde hair set off her crisp, white uniform and her platinum-blonde shoes. She had a perpetual smile that made her look like a fugitive from an unsuccessful toothpaste advertisement. "Yes?"

"I was just wondering what this button does."

"It's a call button. You press it, I come."

"Oh."

The nurse left.

Henry pressed the call button and she came back. "What is it?"

"Should I only press this for something important?"

"Yes," she said, an edge forming on her voice. Her wide smile began to strain at the corners. "Do you need something?"

"No, I was just wondering."

The third time he pressed the call button, she tapped her toe a bit impatiently, carving dents into the solid concrete floor.

"I want ice cream," Henry announced.

"That's for removing your tonsils, not for removing a wand from your nose."

"Is there such a big difference?"

"I could remove your tonsils and show you."

"Um, no thanks," Henry said, starting to notice the nurse's impatience. She left, slamming the door behind her hard enough to rattle the windows and knock the glass out of the TV.

Henry twitched his aching nose. He had learned his lesson far too well to ever, ever underestimate a girl again.

"Hey, Henry. Here you are," Horrendous said, popping her head into the cramped room. "I did your homework, 'cause I know that, since you're the star of the book and all, you don't really have time to do it yourself."

"Hey, thanks. That was really thoughtful. I hope you didn't worry your little head too much about those hard problems. I *am* in *advanced super extra remedial math, kindergarten level, you know.*"

When Henry rang the bell for a fourth time, the nurse came in, valiantly restraining herself from pitching Henry bed and all out of the window. She and the doctor consulted on the best way to remove the wire trashcan that had somehow become wedged on Henry's head. In the end, it took a crowbar, three doctors pushing and pulling, and the assistance of Gallicia Goat, not to mention the emove-ray ashcan-tray spell that had been invented for the Henry Potty Plot Speculations class, which seemed to generate large amounts of trashcan fillings at incredible speeds.

"Thank goodness," said Henry, no longer sounding like a choking whale now that the wastebasket had returned to its previous position by the foot of the bed. "But I have to say, you nurses seem awfully inefficient."

Since the nurse refused to remove the thermometer from Henry's ear, he walked out of the doctor's office feeling rather grumpy, and only able to hear half of the conversations around him.

As he left, he noticed a room marked "Blood Donors." He peeked inside to find a unicorn hooked up to an IV that filtered its blood before sending it to the patient on the other side of the curtain. Getting the strangest feeling that something was wrong, reinforced by the strong odor of garbage in the room, Henry snuck inside and yanked back the curtain.

Lord Revolting lay there, reading a copy of *Time Magazine* with clocks scattered all over the front and back covers. He looked up and saw Henry, who was drawing himself up to make a dramatic statement.

"Time to go," said Revolting, and he vanished, leaving a rather startled unicorn behind.

"This has not been a good day," Henry said. A heap of magically created unwashed laundry promptly plummeted from above and landed on him.

☆ ☆ ☆

Henry stumbled out of the infirmary shaking his head in confusion. Unfortunately, this wasn't enough to dislodge the thermometer.

"Hi, Henry," said a little red haired girl wearing a "We love H. P." button on her shirt. Henry had been handing them out for three weeks both day and night. At last his efforts were paying off and one person was actually wearing one. "Would you sign this for me?" She held out a piece of paper and a pen.

Then she stared at him. Red meshmarks from the wire trashcan checkered his face. His left nostril was swollen to twice its normal size. Shreds of used tissues and toilet paper dotted his hair. A sock and several pairs of boxer shorts were caught in his belt buckle and shoelaces. And a large thermometer stuck out of his right ear.

The little girl pulled the paper back, accidentally pointing the pen straight at Henry. "No, never mind."

Upon seeing a sharp, pointed object in the hands of a female, Henry spun and fled for his life in the opposite direction.

At last he made his way to the mailroom. "There aren't any females in here, are there?" he asked, popping his head into the bustling office. Outside, disgruntled postal workers were busy picketing for better hours and plotting to blow up the world. Inside, gruntled employees sorted letters (and a few numbers).

"In the mailroom?" the postal worker asked. "Of course not, males only. Can we help you?"

Henry didn't want to admit that he was hiding out for fear of offending another girl or woman armed with a sharp object. "Um, I was just looking for a quiet place to sit and study." He plopped down on a chair and picked up a handy issue of *Gizzard's Life*. Suddenly, he dropped his magazine. Lord Revolting stood in front of him! From completely out of nowhere! Yet again! Here Henry was, quietly following Lord Revolting with all of his brilliant investigative talents, and his nemesis kept catching him. Henry felt his mouth drop open in shock, surprise, and a not insignificant amount of pure terror.

Lord Revolting's face screwed up as if he'd tasted something truly disgusting, like the cafeteria's tuna surprise. "Expelli-arms!" Immediately, Henry's arms fell off his shoulders and tumbled to the ground like warm, fleshy toothpicks. Well, longer than toothpicks. And fatter. And there were only two. Alright, toothpicks weren't really the best description. Anyhow, Lord Revolting vanished in a puff of smoke, leaving behind a discarded trail of toilet paper. It was pink.

Henry had never felt so helpless. He couldn't even pick his nose, let alone stop Lord Revolting if he had somehow had the cunning to steal a used postage stamp. Henry sat back down on the bench, staring sadly at his discarded arms.

"Ut-pay em-thay ack-bay!" a voice shouted. Henry blinked in tearful relief as the postal worker came to his rescue. His arms leaped up to their proper positions. "You'd better rest for a moment, and give the superglue a chance to take hold," the worker said sympathetically. "It happens to us all from time to time."

Henry was happy to stay where he was, away from angry females and Lord Revolting's cowardly disarming tactics. He glanced towards the mail slots, wondering if the publishers had accepted his self published copies of his Henry Potty series, translated into various obscure languages to make sure it was available to anyone. Unfortunately, these languages were incredibly strange and mysterious ones such as Latin, Aramaic, and New Yorker.

He could hear feathers fluttering in the breeze and odd snorting sounds. Probably the messenger birds used to send the mail. The snorting grew louder and Henry wondered if the birds had colds. He grimaced, remembering his own miserable doctor's appointment and the thermometer still in his ear. He turned his head to the side and bent over, then started whacking the other side of his head repeatedly, hoping to drive it out.

Henry slammed to the ground right onto his posterior as something swooped out of the sky, dive-bombing towards his head. The interloper thudded onto his chest, snorting and flapping. Henry glanced up to find himself nose to nose with a rather large porker.

"A flying pig?!"

"Oh yes, they're all the rage now," the postal worker explained. "Sorry she landed on you. I guess with you bent over like that, Hortense here thought you were her landing pad."

Hortense snorted pleasantly in Henry's face, presumably unaware of the fact that she weighed two hundred pounds and lay securely on top on Henry. "Get it off me!" he shouted.

"All right, all right, keep your hair on." The postal worker clapped his hands and Hortense rose gracefully into the air. "I think she likes you."

"Perfect! The only female in this school who can stand me right now would have to be a pig! What is that all over this hog, warts?"

"The still ones are. The wriggly ones are fleas. Careful, they're catching."

"Why on earth do you use such horrible creatures?" Henry asked. He kept both eyes on Hortense, who was slowly drifting towards him, long eyelashes batting appealingly. The choking stench of pigpens floated ahead of her.

"Pigs are very intelligent animals. We give them all sorts of fascinating jobs."

Henry took a step back. Hortense was gaining on him. "Like what? Garbage disposal? Refuse eating? Jumping on unsuspecting humans?"

"Hardly. Along with her occasional duties as mailpig, Hortense is one of our finest magical researchers. She translates all our important documents for us."

"What?"

"It's true." The postal worker noticed Henry's wide-eyed stare of confusion. "Don't you see? All of the spells here at Chickenfeet were written in Pig Latin."

"Oh." This actually made a twisted sort of sense. "Well, can you tell her to leave me alone? She's floating closer. It looks as if she's planning to attack me, or lick me, or something gross."

"Stop grumbling; she's just being friendly. See those big hoofprints on your shirt? Hortense only stomps on people she likes."

"Oh, yeah? Well, next time try to miss, Piggy," Henry muttered

He escaped from the post office before Hortense could land on him again, or worse yet, deposit a souvenir of piggly affection from where she floated. Perhaps pigs weren't the best creatures to be flapping above innocent people.

Before Henry left the mail room, he did a secret, mysterious errand while trying to be careful not to draw attention to it, since he didn't want to spoil the book for any of the beloved readers who called him a hero and bought all the Henry Potty autographed toilet seats.

After he'd finished his completely innocuous covert task, once again not calling attention to it, Henry hurried off on another quick errand to the fish market. Walking past Higgle's new Jumbo Hot Dog booth, he paused. Surely that hadn't been there before. And who was that tall gizzard in the black bathrobe hurrying away from the scene? Could it be…Lord Revolting? Surely no one else would have the audacity to wear cat barf in public. Henry fumbled for his wand, realized he didn't have it, and finally shrugged. Didn't the good guy get to screw up once or twice and fail to catch the villain? He hoped so.

Henry's stomach growled, reminding him that it was one of his few body parts which hadn't been abused in the past few hours. "I just wish I could figure out what happened to my wand," he muttered, getting in line. Henry bought a hot dog, heroically gesturing for Higgle to keep the change. He ducked as the blinding white light of his conscience shone down again. It hit Higgle straight in the eyes, making him howl and squirt Henry with the extra mustard he'd ordered. Henry stared down at the yellow circle on his black bathrobe, complete with a few strategic dabs in the center. "Very artistic, Higgle," he said, admiring the new smiley face.

He passed straight by the eempa-lecmpas, a crowd of small, little men. (This isn't being repetitive; these men were so tiny that they needed both adjectives. In fact, they were rather difficult to locate if you didn't have a magnifying glass handy. After the twentieth or thirtieth eempa-leempa was fried to death while someone attempted to find them and give them orders, a motion was passed that they would wear red shirts and wave little flags whenever they saw the big people coming. The flags were doubly useful since, if someone wanted a hanky, they just had to grab one. Anyway…) The eempa-leempas filled the candy machines, mopped the floors, and walked the Chickenfeet mascot, an overweight ostrich named George. Henry carefully strolled around them. The last time someone had stepped on an eempa-leempa, their whole colony had been so upset that they'd filled all the candy machines with sprouts and artichokes. Henry shuddered at the memory.

☆ ☆ ☆

As he continued his walk back to the dorms and safety, Henry noticed a pile of children scrabbling in the brook. Half of them wore red shirts and the other half wore yellow. These colors went nicely with their bright blue faces from trying to drown each other in the freezing water.

"What are you playing?" Henry asked.

One of the gasping teammates crawled out of the mayhem to lie exhausted on the riverbank. "It's called Quick-grab-the-fish. The object is to grab the fish. We need to find the little gold one."

"Sounds simple enough," Henry said. "I'm Henry Potty, the star of the book. Can I play?"

"I'm John Johnson, and these are Will Wilson, Vladimir Vladimirson, and Susan Susanson. Sure you can join; we could use someone small to stand on. And we always need someone to be picked last." Seeing Henry's sudden discouragement, John added, "But, hey, being picked last means you're the best. Dunno how it works in England. Just watch out for the sharks that swim around in here. That's how we lost the last three players."

"Why do you have sharks in the river?"

"It's exciting, of course!"

"Oh, well, if it's exciting. Sounds like fun."

"So are you in or out?"

"I'm in," Henry said, matching his words by diving into the freezing water. Immediately, he could feel his extremities growing numb, as a prelude to falling off. Waves dashed against his face and cut off his air supply. A frightened fish swam up his nose. The game grew better by the minute.

A few seconds later, Henry yelled, "I got it, I got it!" He held up a struggling fish, failing to notice that it was the wrong color.

"Nope," Susan said. "You only got a red herring."

Chapter 4:

CLASSROOM CALAMITIES

Come on, Henry, it's time for classes," Horrendous said eagerly. Henry stared at her. All he could see was an enormous pile of textbooks with two feet sticking out the bottom. Her purple sock didn't match the green stripy one. At least, he didn't think it did.

"But I don't need to go to classes," Henry protested. "Why do I need grades? My job is to be the star of the book."

"People like to read about things they can identify with," Horrendous said. "All children have to go to classes, do homework, and eat sprouts. It's part of their boring, ungizzardly lives. So you have to do it too, to set a good example. Have you written your essay on 'Who I Enchanted Over My Summer Vacation?' It's due today."

"Oh, I, um, didn't enchant anyone," Henry replied after thinking it over for several minutes. These were actual minutes as opposed to the "wait a minute" sort of minute.

"Well, you need to come up with an essay somehow."

Horrendous left the room in search of her pocket protector, trustingly leaving her completed essay on the bed. A moment later she returned and picked it up, failing to notice that it now read, "Now On Sale: Henry Potty Action Figures. Comes with realistic tripping over own shoelaces action as well as a free comic book. Buy Now!" She also didn't notice the bulge in Henry's pocket.

"First, we're going to try the spell of levitation," the teacher of Magic 101 said a few minutes later. A ghost who'd refused to leave his body behind, he dragged the festering, twenty-year-old corpse with him everywhere. He always had a large entourage of flies, and his students frequently carried nose plugs with them to class. Ghosts had significant trouble picking anything up with foggy fingers, so he had to rely on using his spooky, light up vision as a pointer. Luckily, this only set the wall on fire now and then.

"Everyone point your wand at your book." Horrendous aimed her wand at her pile of textbooks. Henry placed his book on top of Really Wimpy's. "Now everyone speak the magic words. Ick-pay is-thay up-way!"

Everyone dutifully recited the magic words. The teacher made his way around the classroom. "Excellent, Henry, it seems that your book rose the highest." Henry smiled and tried to look nonchalant while Really Wimpy sweated over trying to lift two books into the air. The teacher moved on to Horrendous.

"Miss Gangrene, this looks very disappointing," he said. Horrendous's immense pile of textbooks failed to budge, no matter how much she grunted and repeated the magic charm.

Henry glanced at her sympathetically from behind Really Wimpy's desk. "Hey, that's the breaks, I guess."

Unfortunately, Bumbling Bore taught the next class. Within twenty seconds, all heads except Horrendous's had made smacking noises as they hit the desks.

Really Wimpy jerked to a sitting position as Henry elbowed him in the ribs. "Time for recess!" Really shouted, jumping to his feet. Everyone jerked awake at this latest announcement. However, before they could stampede towards the door, Bumbling Bore hit the emergency button behind his desk. Immediately, a bullet proof, ten-inch thick iron door dropped down between the students and their gateway to freedom.

"It is NOT time to leave," Bumbling Bore said firmly. "Mr. Wimpy, I'm surprised at you. I would expect this sort of cavalier, flying in the face of authority behavior from, say, Mr. Potty. He's the hero and heroes never listen to their teachers. They spend the entire story disobeying rules and magically end up with straight A's. Well, not in my class. Here, you're going to listen."

Bumbling Bore looked sternly at Henry, who dragged his head up, suddenly aware of the teacher's gaze. "Hmm?"

"Both looking up and asking questions. Excellent progress. Now, you can all go back to doodling or comparing the length of your nostril hairs or whatever while I continue to drone…

Twenty minutes later, Henry jerked into a sitting position. Everyone was asleep, sound in their chairs. Bumbling Bore also snoozed, blissfully oblivious to his class's inattention. Henry sprang to his feet. This was his big chance!

"Henry! What are you doing?"

Henry sighed as he turned around slowly. He should have known that Horrendous would be awake. She sat at a perfect ninety-degree angle, pencil resting one inch above the paper as she waited for her teacher to awaken and continue lecturing.

"I'm going to open up the door and escape while he's asleep. Got a problem with that?"

"Of course I have! You'll get us into trouble."

"I know." Henry gave her his best devilish-yet-irresistible smile. "It's my job."

Henry snuck up to the desk, poking only his eyes and tuft of unruly hair out from behind desks, wastebaskets, and his sleeping peers. Then he froze. He waited a moment and Mission: Completely Improbable music floated out of thin air. Much better. Now he just needed some lasers shooting across the room.

Suddenly, two small, beady tracking devices caught him from across the classroom and held him captive as the teacher's eyes opened. Bumbling Bore was awake!

"Henry? What are you doing?" he asked in a deceptively mild voice.

"I'm, um, that is…" Henry frantically searched for a groveling compliment, but none was at hand. He'd left his *Blockhead's Guide to Groveling Compliments for Teachers* in his desk.

"You were going to press the button here and escape, weren't you?"

"Well, er, I…" Behind him, Horrendous waved a bright green pennant with the words "Punish Him" on it.

"My boy, that's splendid! Utterly splendid!"

"Huh?" Henry asked, now at a complete loss for words.

"You understood my lecture on the prison riot of twelve-sixty-four so well that you decided to recreate it. Horrendous, I notice you're not participating. I shall just have to make some notes in my grade book."

Henry shrugged. "Guess that's the breaks, Horrendous."

Horrendous's response has been left out of this book, for fear of blistering the paper.

Cooking class was cancelled, on account of Professor Snort's bad cold. He was sneezing his head off and no one could find the superglue to reattach it. Luckily, Miss McGonk found that she could squeeze them in early to "Real Magic Tricks" if she transformed her other class into lab mice.

"All right," said Miss McGonk, hastily shoving a few last handfuls of cookies down her gullet and speaking with her mouth full. "Now we will study transformations. They're very simple. You point your wand at an object and say what you want it to turn into." Immediately, thirty wands pointed at the professor. "No! Don't transform me!" she said. "Anyone who does gets an F!" Finally, the wands pointed away.

"For goodness sakes! Perhaps we should start with the basics," Miss McGonk muttered. "What does the spell 'Abracadabra' do?" With a puff of green smoke, an overweight penguin in hot pink surfer shorts appeared behind her, a bemused expression on his face.

"I know!" Horrendous called.

"Yes, Horrendous, of course you do. However, I've decided to make it my policy this year to call on the dumb students first so they don't feel left out. Let's see. Miss Muffet?"

"I have no idea." Miffie was too busy constructing a Henry Potty Fan Club tripwire under her desk to pay attention to anything that the teacher had been saying. Presumably it would work as well on its maker as anyone else, especially considering Henry's intelligence compared with, say, a not overly bright cheese sandwich.

"Mr. Potty?"

"Snakes." Henry didn't actually know the answer, but he remembered half-hearing the teacher mention good snakes or something like that a while earlier and it was worth a shot.

"Eek!" Miffie shrieked.

"What's wrong?" Horrendous asked.

"I hate snakes."

Henry nudged Really Wimpy. "Are you thinking what I'm thinking?"

"I think so, Henry," Really Wimpy said. "But I don't know how to find out how peanuts get inside those shells."

Henry shook his head adamantly. "No, not that! I know how to get Miffie back for shoving a wand up my nose!" He paused dramatically. "We'll show her a snake!"

Before Henry could continue with his brilliant plotting, it was time for lunch. All of the children herded from the room and into the cafeteria, like cockroaches going to the slaughter. The Chickenfeet cafeteria was a place of nightmares. Horrifying rumors were all that exited the place, since visiting skunks, vultures, and juicy earthworms were never heard from again. Cats howled in mourning in the alleys outside. The French fries were green and the canned peas not to be viewed by the fainthearted. Many dishes were blanketed in thick, red sauce to disguise the taste, smell, appearance, and sounds that emanated from the food, as well as numbing the stomach lining to better absorb poisonous shocks. Still, it was a break from sandwiches.

From across the cafeteria, Really Wimpy beckoned mysteriously to Miffie.

She lowered her menu with its emergency stomach pumping instructions emblazoned on the back.

"Yes?" she asked. "Why are you beckoning mysteriously, little first year?"

"Hey, Miffie, look at this!" Really Wimpy said. He reached down onto his plate and picked up what he hoped would scare her to death. Or at least make her snort milk up her nose.

Miffie shrugged. "So?"

Henry elbowed his dimwitted friend. "I said a snake, not a steak! Any vampire in town would run away from that moldy thing, but not a student."

"Oh, right." Really Wimpy placed the lump of nearly fossilized meat back on his plate, trying not to get it in the mashed turnips with red sauce. "Guess we need a new brilliant plan to get even with our arch-nemesis."

Henry's brow furrowed with worry. "Maybe we should just let her win this round while we go get a soda."

"Okay, I like that plan."

Henry nodded. "Soda I." He ducked. The mashed turnips soared over his head to smack into Miffie as she returned to her seat. The heavy tray knocked her to the ground, even as the food charred her skin with its acidity. Her scream rang through the cafeteria. "Argh! I'm melting!"

"That's one less arch-nemesis," Henry said.

"Henry! You made that pun just so I'd attack you with my lunch? That's brilliant."

"Of course," Henry said modestly. "I would never make such a bad pun except to attack someone. It's too big a punishment."

Really Wimpy shuddered. "I hope lunch ends soon."

In animal care, the teacher had been recruited from a poodle grooming plantation, in the hopes that he would brush and curl the fur on the cafeteria rats, convince trolls in the Scary Woods to neatly bury the mangled corpses of their victims, mop up after the Vomiting Willow, and otherwise improve the cleanliness of Chickenfeet Academy. He kept his long, purple hair nearly as curled and fluffed as the poodles that he attended to. When the children arrived, he presented each of them with an adorable little chipmunk. "These are no ordinary chipmunks," Professor Flopsie intoned. "These fiercely intelligent creatures will steal everything you have, down to your underwear. For these are technically cheap-munks, and they refuse to pay for anything. Feed them nuts and seeds, but nothing too rich for their delicate little stomachs. If yours dies, you lose."

"Henry, what're you doing?" Horrendous screeched.

"Huh?" Henry glanced up from where he held his peanut-butter sandwich out to the cheap-munk beside him. The cheap-munk took advantage of Henry's distraction to gulp down the rest of his sandwich in one bite. The teacher came by and glanced about.

"Well, Henry, your creature looks happy enough. At least it's not complaining."

The peanut butter had glued its jaws together.

"But, sir, cheap-munks don't talk!" Horrendous protested.

"There you go again, Horrendous, always correcting the teacher," their professor said. "Maybe you'd like to teach the class?"

Horrendous's eyes lit up like two flashbulbs. "Okay!"

"No, no, I didn't mean—that is, you're not supposed to say—oh, go groom your cheap-munk."

"But it is groomed, professor. See how I brushed its fur?"

The professor picked up the cheap-munk with the tips of his long, aristocratic fingers and dumped it in a mud puddle. "Groom it again."

Henry's cheap-munk waxed fat and happy on its irregular diet, while Horrendous's got tired of her lecturing and wandered away. The children's grades came as no surprise to anyone.

Next was charms class. Apparently, the point was to learn charming behavior. Mrs. Goobenshplatzit had golden hair and golden eyes, which set off her equally golden tan. She hailed from Florida, where she spent her days relaxing in the sun and her nights fighting vampires disguised as lifeguards. In fact, she spent so much time relaxing on the beach that the students had named her "the Sand Which."

Henry felt his hands sweat as he stood up to take their oral quiz. "Mrs. Goobenshplatzit, I am..." What was that word? "I am horif—" Henry's aura flickered and he quickly changed his mind. "Honored to meet you." The light continued shining and Henry knew he was saying the right thing.

"But how will this help us learn magic?" Horrendous asked.

"Tsk tsk," the Sand Which said. "You're supposed to say 'excuse me.'" She pressed a button behind her desk. Immediately, a trap door opened under Horrendous and she plummeted into the basement, shrieking as she fell.

Horrendous stumbled into the next class a few minutes late, arms laden with dust-covered textbooks. No one dared to comment, not even Henry. They were too afraid that she'd pulverize them with a glare.

"Welcome to Defense from Darkness," Miss Ann Thropist said. She stood at the front of the class, swirling gray robe set off by a fringed vest and trendy, white cowgirl hat. She was quite expert in teaching the children how to fight darkness and evil, since she was the most evil person who had ever lived. Over the summer and on weekends, that was. The rest of the year, she operated a trendy clothes shop. She was known to most of her students as "The Wicked Which of the Vest."

"We will be studying that most important of skills, how to turn on flashlights! Ready, now!"

The classroom filled with rays of fifty watt bulbs.

"Horrendous? I don't see any light at all from yours. And everyone told me you were a bright student."

"Please, Ma'am, I gave the batteries to the little starving orphans standing outside, so that they could at least play with their handheld video games while they beg for food."

"Well, that's an automatic F for you. Henry, did you want to say anything?"

Henry's hand waved frantically, stretching towards the ceiling. "May I say, I've never had a teacher as beautiful as you are." A warm, white glow beamed through the room, thanks to Henry's conscience.

"Well, that'll be an A for the light, plus a bonus for kissing up to the teacher," said the wicked which. "Now, I should go. Some malodorous hooded figure in green makeup requested a meeting."

"But that's not fair," Horrendous protested.

Henry shrugged. "That's the breaks."

"No," Horrendous said sweetly. "This is!" She brought his flashlight and all its batteries heavily down on his hollow skull with a resounding clunk.

Finally, the children arrived at their last class of the day.

"Ah, herbology," Horrendous said. "Finally something I'm good at."

"Actually, the class has changed this year to hobology, that is, the study of hobos," their teacher announced.

"That's great." Henry said. "I'm going to be a professional hobo."

Horrendous dropped her head onto her folded arms. "Oh, brother!"

☆ ☆ ☆

The next day, Really Wimpy sat down next to Henry in cooking class and passed him something under the table.

"What's this?" He whispered to make sure he didn't disturb the teacher busy snoring in the front of the room. Professor Snort was still recovering from his monumental cold, and had made it clear that anyone caught waking him up would be in an enormous pile of pig poo. Remembering the postal pigs, Henry had to shudder.

"Exploding gum. You chew it until it's soft, and then drop it front of someone you don't like. About five seconds later, it explodes."

"Really, you're a genius!" Henry popped the gum into his mouth and began chomping.

"No, it's sold in the cafeteria, and the label says, "Get rid of little annoying girls with cutesy names." I figured we might be able to think of someone who fit that description, if we both tried hard enough. Or we could use it on Miffie when she comes back to class, since the steak idea didn't pan out." Miffie was off having medical technicians scrape the hideous mass of turnips off her face, and getting a nose job while she was at it.

Henry rolled his eyes and didn't say anything. He noticed that the cute little redhead who'd wanted his autograph was sitting on the other side of the room. He blew a bubble, hoping to attract her with his childish charm. Nothing. He blew a second, bigger bubble. This time she smiled a bit. Henry was so busy gazing into her eyes that he completely forgot about the bubble, which grew to monumental proportions, then suddenly popped over all of his face.

"Potty! What did I say about waking me up!" Professor Snort thundered. However, Henry suddenly remembered that he had a bigger problem than his teacher or even Hortense Hog. The exploding gum was plastered all over his face and he had only a few seconds to remove it. He desperately tore at the sticky goo, trying to dislodge it before the gum exploded. He finally tugged away a double handful of the nasty stuff, rolled it up, and threw it as far away from himself as he could manage. Unfortunately, the direction he picked was that of the professor.

Henry had to wait for a very long time before Bumbling Bore finally let him escape. The lecture dragged on for four hours, explaining in great detail how strict the rules were for unsuccessfully trying to kill a teacher. It had been the most mind-numbing exercise Henry had ever encountered. In Henry's opinion, he had more than paid for what, after all, had been an accidental attempt to kill the teacher. But Professor Snort wasn't buying it. He sentenced Henry to the worst punishment he could think of: skipping lunch to launder his hankies. Of course, after he'd started, Henry didn't want lunch. In fact, he never wanted to see food again.

"Sheesh," Really Wimpy said as they scurried down the hall towards their newest class. "All that for blowing a bubble at the wrong time."

Henry was still green around his nonexistent gills. "I know," Henry sighed. "But I'd give anything for that little redheaded girl to notice me." He smoothed the yellow shirt that had been white before Professor Snort's punishment. A black zigzag marked where the electric hanky dryer had attacked him with its dreaded laser vision. "If I worry about this any more, I may go bald from the strain."

"Well, that would be strange," Really said, not paying much attention, since they'd arrived at their absolutely last class, Suicide Made Easy 101. After twelve students had gotten killed on the first day, some spaces had opened on the wait list. All of the students' homework had disappeared the day before (probably eaten by ambitious cheap-munks). In a fit of pique, Professor Flopsie had suspended the children from animal care and ordered them to go jump off a cliff. This class qualified.

Horrendous had been the first to join, eager to pile another class onto her busy schedule. This time she felt enthusiastic about Henry succeeding more than she did. The boys wandered to the edge of Chickenfeet lawn, which was already covered with sharp objects such as spikes, beds of nails, and strong Swiss cheese.

Miss McGonk tapped her foot and crossed her arms. "Well, come closer. You won't get hurt standing on the edge of the field." She raised her wand, ready to transform the pair of them into feather dusters if they seemed likely to escape her den of tortures. Miss McGonk gestured to an untidy heap of appliances, three of them bent and twisted beyond recognition. "Here you are, students, your first vacuum cleaners. Now I'm going to walk conveniently out of hearing range for a few minutes. I don't want anyone touching the vacuums."

She jostled Henry, who was staring out into space. "No one touches them, am I clear?"

"Of course, Miss McGonk," Henry said, trying to look as if he knew what he was saying yes to.

"Good."

The moment that Miss McGonk had left, Henry grabbed the biggest vacuum.

"What are you doing!" Horrendous screeched. "She'll grind you into mincemeat and bake you—you're not supposed to ride it yet. We have to wait for her to show us."

"I can't help it—it's like I've got this giant vacuum between my ears, begging me to try this."

As Henry soared into the clouds, Horrendous grimaced. "You've sure got that right."

When Henry finally landed, he staggered past his waiting classmates towards Professor McGonk. "Um…maybe you were right," he said. As his face turned even greener than it had been before his flight, he suddenly threw up all over her shoes.

Henry burped. "Ah, much better!"

"Potty! You're in big trouble now. Nobody heaves on the professor's shoes without getting detention. I'm assigning you to trim the Chickenfeet toenails and give them a manicure."

Henry turned even greener, and upchucked a second time. Miss McGonk closed her eyes briefly, in a mild appeal to heaven. Heaven, as usual, wasn't responding. Her feet were rather buried, and smelling enough to curdle the glass shards shining on the lawn. "For the next three weeks, you get to shovel out the stables of the big-bottomed sludge monsters!"

Henry gulped in air, paused, straightened, and then suddenly bent over and blew his cookies a third time.

Miss McGonk dodged aside and managed to avoid any further insult to her shoes. "All right, Potty, that's it! For this, you get to be our Quick-grab-the-fish Sneezer!"

Chapter 5:

THE PARROT AND THE GUM

The Sneezer's job, as it turned out, was to grab the goldfish first, and then hold onto it while everyone else dogpiled on top of him. Miss McGonk hadn't let him leave until after she'd called Triple V to have her vacuum insurance updated. They had left her crystal ball on hold for over an hour while Henry attempted to Sneeze his way through the cold, slippery game. To make things worse, the fish kept swatting him in the face with their tails. He'd promised them over and over to eat chicken forever and forego seafood, but it hadn't seemed to make a dent in their slippery abuse. Wet, shivering, and sore, Henry finally dripped his way back to the dormitory. His hand tightly clutched his only lifeline, the book *Fishing for Nincompoops.*

"Password?" the fat lady asked sweetly.

Henry hesitated, trying to think through all the water in his ears.

"That's right, go on inside!"

"What?" asked Henry. "I didn't say anything."

"Exactly. The password is to make a sound like a lump of leftover spinach. And you got it!"

Henry shrugged and hurried inside before the portrait could change her mind.

☆ ☆ ☆

As Henry ran to lunch, having put on dry clothes and combed a fraction of the mud, fish guts and student guts out of his hair, he heard someone screaming inside one of the classrooms. It sounded as if they were saying, "No, no, please have mercy! Don't make me agree to this. I can't. I just can't!"

Henry poked his head inside. "Don't fear! I have my evil gizzard squirt gun all ready!" He glanced around. Professor Flopsie, the ex-poodle groomer, sat alone at his desk. "I don't get it. Where's Lord Revolting?"

"Don't say that name!"

Henry rolled his eyes. "Okay, okay, where's You-know-who?"

"Oh. He's not here. Why? Do you see him? Do you see him anywhere?"

"Um, no," Henry said.

"Good. I was talking to…myself. Yes, that's it, to myself. No one here, go right on about your business."

"Oh, good, glad I could help." Henry left, grinning. Obviously, he had frightened Revolting away from the school, just by staying out of his way. Henry had forgotten to look under the rug.

Bumbling Bore's office was opposite the cafeteria, so that he could instantly prevent riots protesting the disgustingness of the food. As Henry passed, the principal beckoned to him mysteriously from the door of his office. "Henry, I have something to give to you." He motioned for Henry to follow him, leading him through twisting corridors and passageways, then right back to his office when he absentmindedly took a wrong turn. "Come in, come in! Now where did I put it? I always have trouble finding the dratted thing."

Henry glanced about the room. The place was a junk heap. Empty suntan lotion bottles and red lifeguard shorts lay scattered about. A few shirts in different colors all read, "My not-so-great-grandkids went somewhere exotic and all they brought me was this dumb shirt." There was a wobbling stack of CDs, all by the Beetles, a group of former musicians who had been changed into insects by a gizzard who wished they'd turn down all that racket. There were also manacles, whips, muzzles, and all the usual instruments of torture to be found in a principal's office. Of course, for extreme disciplinary measures, rumor had it that the teacher kept a video on how to paint, wallpaper, and reupholster one's house. For repeat offenders, there was *The History of Cabbages* in Polish.

"Oh, by the way, here's your wand," Bumbling Bore said, handing it over. The tip was bent and it smelled strongly of hot dogs. "I couldn't allow an uneducated adult to go around using it, not when we had so many perfectly qualified students who would only ever use wands to facilitate learning."

"Of course," Henry said, using the wand to scratch his back. It sent a stream of sparks down his robe, adding orange polka dots and a "Kick Me" sign to the back, but Henry didn't notice.

Bumbling Bore resumed his search through his desk. Henry yawned and leaned against the perch of the headmaster's pet parrot, Socks. "Polly want a cracker?" he asked the bird.

"Well, all right, you can have one, but only if you flap your wings and do a little dance," the bird muttered in an entirely unmusical voice. Fingernails on a blackboard would have been opera in comparison.

"No, I meant do you want one?"

"Hello! Birds eat birdseed. Crackers are for numbskull humans like you. And you don't even have a cracker if I did want one. Complete bad manners if you ask me. Who are you, anyway?"

"I'm Henry Potty, the star of the book." Henry drew himself up and gave the bird his brilliant trademark grin, guaranteed to have little girls fainting at his feet. Come to think of it, not many girls had been fainting lately. His presence hadn't produced so much as an embarrassed giggle. Although there had been six attacks of gas. It was a start.

"Well, I didn't vote for you," she said. "I'm sure I'm far more important than some smelly little boy who can't even hold onto his magic wand."

Henry struggled for a snappy comeback, but it was horribly slow in arriving. He thought for so long that Bumbling Bore finally finished sorting through his enormous desk. The principal straightened, brushing aside paper clips, hearing aids, memos suggesting that he retire, and evil gizzards' charred skulls cluttering up the unseen surface. "Aha! Here it is."

Henry turned, and found that the headmaster carefully cradled something in his hands. The only problem was that his hands were empty. That's it, Henry thought. The headmaster's finally gone senile.

I wonder if the parrot would tell on me if I raided his desk. I'll bet there's all sorts of cool gizzarding stuff in there, or at least a new pencil sharpener. I definitely need one after Really Wimpy tried sharpening his rock with the old one.

Unfortunately for Henry's pencils, Bumbling Bore hadn't yet gone any more senile than he already was. "It's an invisibility cloak!" Bumbling Bore announced. "It always takes me forever to find. You'd think the makers could put labels or purple stripes or something on it. But no, completely invisible."

"Why are you giving it to me?" Henry asked, so excited that he forgot to fall asleep at Bumbling Bore's announcement. Finally, something he could use to completely revenge herself on Miffie Muffet instead of the exploding gum. At the least, he could make all sorts of snack raids on the kitchen. While the food wasn't edible, it would make fine ammunition against his unsuspecting classmates.

"It belonged to your ancestors, generations ago. It's a sort of family heirloom, passed down from father to son."

"Like my dad's receding hairline," Henry breathed in awe. "But wait, if it's my family heirloom, why do you have it?"

Bumbling Bore coughed into his beard. "Oh, er, that. Well, I... acquired it years ago, under circumstances too long and intricate to go into in great detail. I didn't think anyone would miss it; the cloak's invisible, after all. And it's been quite useful for checking out the women's locker— er, that is, the women's soccer team."

"You mean football," Henry corrected. "Isn't this supposed to be a British book?"

"No, no, not this one," Bumbling Bore said. "Our readers are stuck with the Americanized version, everything translated and whirled in a blender until it's mindless pabulum, perfectly fit for American minds."

"Oh," Henry said. "What's a blender?"

Bumbling Bore began a lecture about modern children and their lack of intelligence, woeful musical taste, hopelessness at styling their hair, and general inability to poach eggs. Somewhere in the middle of it, Henry dozed into blissful slumber. He awoke to find the room empty, save for Socks the parrot, who was busy industriously pecking a hole in the invisibility cloak.

"Now my belly button will show," Henry protested as he reclaimed the shredded fabric.

The parrot shrugged, as much as any bird can shrug at least. "Better that than your face, moron."

"Why do you keep insulting me?" Henry asked. "Can't you handle the fact that I'm more famous than you are? Or is it some disguised attempt to be friendly, creating a bridge between us with what you think are funny comments?"

"Nothing so complex, toast for brains. I'm only half parrot. My mother was a mocking bird!"

In Defense from Darkness class later that day, Henry tried using his magical cloak to sneak out. Bumbling Bore hadn't told him how to use it, after all. However, since the class was conducted in pitch-blackness, being invisible wasn't that much of an advantage. Miss Ann Thropist caught him when Henry opened the door and let the light in, and she punished Henry by forcing him to stay after school and pound erasers.

"The one thing I don't understand," Henry muttered rebelliously as he filled the hall with chalk dust. "Is why a class that's conducted in pitch darkness needs a *black*board."

The Scary Woods was the only place to find magical mushrooms. Students had been forbidden to go there, ever since a little blond girl in a blue dress had eaten a dozen of those fickle fungi, and grown large enough to crush half of Chickenfeet with a single stomp of her size 93 shoe. The girl had gone on to become quite a famous actress, starring in movies such as *Bride of King Kong*, and *Sleepless With Godzilla*, but Chickenfeet was still recovering from its squashing.

Henry decided to enter the forest despite the school rules. At that very minute, Lord Revolting could be plucking every magical mushroom in the place, safe from the eyes of everyone except the resident blind bats. Henry couldn't let his struggle to avoid failing all his classes keep him from his greater mission to stop Lord Revolting from completing his devilish schemes. He invited Really Wimpy to go, but at the word "scary," Really had retreated under the bed, not to be heard from until dinnertime. Henry tiptoed through Chickenfeet,

51

invisibility cloak folded under his arm. He only realized he'd made a mistake when a bony, clawlike hand snatched the back of his jacket.

He spun around to find that the creature holding him was…not that terrifying, actually.

"Now, I've got you, you little sneak!" Filth said. "Vigilance is my middle name."

Henry thought furiously. For once in his life, the tiniest gem of an idea seemed to be blossoming in his head. He concentrated, and his thought processes clicked on after only ten minutes of standing motionless, while the book considerately paused to let him summon his thoughts. "You know, Mr. Filth, I think you're really a wonderful person."

"What?" asked Filth. He wasn't used to compliments. "Filth, we think you're a slimeball and even worms wouldn't crawl on you," all right, that was a typical greeting as far as he was concerned. But flattery?

Henry's good deed aura glowed around him as he continued. "Yes, sir, I think you're really swell." The aura continued to brighten. "In fact," Henry said, stretching his arms out for a big hug, "I think I love you!"

As Filth's eyes widened in shock, the light from Henry's now brilliant aura struck him full in the face. Temporarily blinded and thoroughly perplexed, he stood frozen as a leftover corndog forgotten in the back of the freezer. Henry gleefully made his escape and snuck down the corridor. A moment later he stopped, paused, blinked, shook his head, considered for a moment, smiled, and put on his invisibility cloak. Around the corner, he could hear an odd collection of sounds. Mingled thumps and soft cawing put him in mind of a crow being mashed against a wall with a marble pastry board. Still, Henry was busy enough chasing Lord Revolting without being distracted by random clues. He drew up his invisible hood and left the academy.

Henry snuck into the Scary Woods. He wore his invisibility cloak, leaving him completely impervious to detection except for his tennis shoes (the cloak was rather short) and his belly button.

Suddenly, he saw Lord Revolting in front of him, his pockets stuffed with something lumpy. As usual, the evil gizzard smelled like the hind end of a grouchy hippo. "So, Henry Potty! We meet again."

"How'd you know it was me?" Henry asked.

"I know your shoe size."

Henry suddenly realized that he was standing in front of his hated enemy, the archvillain of the book, the man who'd flushed his goldfish. He pushed back his cloak, and then drew his wand, careful not to get it caught in his bathrobe and ruin the dramatic moment. "Hello. My name is Henry Potty. You killed my goldfish. Prepare to die."

Lord Revolting raised his wand with one hand and made a little flicking gesture with the other. Immediately, Henry's wand flew away, and landed in the bushes some distance off.

"Um, did I say prepare to die?" Henry asked. "I meant prepared to be injured. Slightly injured. Prepare to be treated very nicely and sent on your way, that's what I meant to say."

"Oh, don't worry," Lord Revolting said to him. "I'm not here to kill you. I have something far more terrible in mind. I'm going to spoil the book again!"

"No!" Henry said. He put his fingers in his ears and started singing as loud as he could. "This is the song that never ends! It goes on and on, my friends. Some people started singing it, not knowing what it was. And they continued singing it forever just because, this is the song that never ends! It goes on and on, my friends. Some people started singing it, not knowing what it was. And they continued singing it forever just because, this is the song that—"

"Stop it, stop it," Lord Revolting shouted over Henry's horrible singing. The boy's voice grated like a wire brush on the inside of a soup tureen. Overhead, birds were tumbling from their perches, shrieking in agony. The lucky ones knocked themselves unconscious on the ground. "Stop it, I said!" Henry sang the next four identical verses even louder. "All right, all right, I'm leaving."

"You are?" Henry asked, removing his hands from his ears.

"Yes. But first I wanted to tell you...someone you care about will die! Either that or you'll swallow your gum. Have a nice day." He brought his hand down in a firm, dramatic gesture, and a puff of smoke appeared out of nowhere and enveloped him.

Henry quietly watched. After a moment, the smoke dissipated to reveal Lord Revolting standing exactly where he'd been before. "My Great-Aunt Susie's spotted underwear!" Revolting yelled. He waved his hand in a furious gesture. Immediately, Henry's shoelaces

53

tied themselves together. Then Lord Revolting stomped rather less dramatically out of the forest.

"Hey! Psst, kid!" a voice called from the undergrowth. Henry glanced around hopefully. He'd been standing there for over an hour, unable to move with his shoelaces tied.

A grizzled head peeped out from the undergrowth. The owner hadn't shaved in months, by the look of him. He wore bell-bottoms, or rather, a bell-bottomed shirt. He couldn't wear bell-bottomed trousers, owing to the fact that his lower half was a giraffe. Rhinestones sparkled in his hair and a distinct odor of magical mushroom floated from his unwashed clothing. He carried a Ouija board, star chart, and a magic decoder ring from a cereal box.

"Got a tip for ya, man: after you destroy the evil ring—"

"What evil ring?"

"No one gave you an evil ring?"

Henry shook his head.

"How about a magic sword? Been in any churchyards lately?"

"No."

"Oh, I see. You're the new hope, the chosen one who will defeat the evil empire, the sky wa—"

"Um, no, you've got the wrong person. I'm Henry Potty. Would you like an authentic Henry Potty talking stuffed animal? It's a porcupine. Please, don't ask why. Just pull the string and it says 'Would you like an autograph?'"

"Wow, that sounds groovy, man! But if I got a new toy, all the other mystical gurus would feel totally jealous. We're like, the Star Gazers. And we've got a present for you!" He held out a box, neatly wrapped in several layers of tape labeled "YoU'll nede this 'n ChuPter Sevn."

"Um, thanks," Henry said. He took the box. It struggled slightly in his arms, emitting a soft yowling noise. "What's in this? And how will it help me?"

"Nice try." The creature grinned. "No one is ever supposed to tell the hero what magical gifts are good for. Us ordinary folk just mysteriously show up, give you the Holy Three-Ton Tomato of Sacrifice or something, mutter a few cryptic phrases and slink off again. Then we hide under the nearest rock and hope that if you blow yourself up, you at least won't make too much of a mess. We had quite a mound of spaghetti less than a week after the last tomato bestowing.

Henry sifted through this last exchange for useful facts, but couldn't find any. "Could you please untie my shoelaces?"

The strange centaur shook his head. "Sorry, dude, we're like, sworn not to interfere."

"Wait a minute! What about this box?"

"Oh that's not interfering, dude, that's bribery. See, after you dodge through the world of plumbing and septic tanks to rescue the princess—"

"Never mind. But can you help me? I'm stuck!"

The Star Gazer shrugged. "Better hop something comes up."

"Hello, Henry. How's your day been?" Horrendous asked. Henry sat on the floor, six fingers, one ear and his nose all tangled in his shoelaces as he furiously tried to bite them apart. Unaware that the end of the previous scene contained a small typo, Henry had accordingly hopped back to his room. It was the recently polished stairs with Goober's Extra Greasy Polishing Oil that'd been the nasty part.

Horrendous waved her wand over him. "Untie-way Is-thay incompoop-nay!"

Henry did his best not to look too relieved as the shoelaces loosed their ferocious grasp on him. He crossed his legs and pretended that he was perfectly comfortable on the floor and had only been wrestling with his shoelaces for the heck of it. "Oh, just fine, Horrendous. First, I got up and watched Wand-y Tunes on TV. Then Lord Revolting turned up and told me one of my friends would die. How've you been?"

"One of your friends? But that could be me! Or Really Wimpy! We have to do something. Tell me, what did he say, exactly?"

"He said that he was going to spoil the book for me, and that either someone I cared about would die, or I'd swallow my gum."

"That's terrible!"

"Yeah, I know. Everyone says that when you swallow gum, it sticks around in your stomach and collects in a big—"

"I meant the part about someone dying!"

"Oh, yeah, that's what I meant, too."

"So what do we plan to do?"

"Take bets? I mean, if Really Wimpy dies, we could share his pet rock. I could have him Mondays and Thursdays, while—"

"Henry!"

"What?" he asked, blinking in an oblivious manner. "On the other hand, if Bumbling Bore bought it, maybe I could become a professor—"

"It's always about you, isn't it?"

"Of course. Remember, Horrendous, I'm a star."

"I just need a good idea," Horrendous muttered. "Bingo!"

"And I was so close," Henry muttered, dropping his bingo board.

"No, I know how to avoid Lord Revolting's plans. He said someone would die *or* you'd swallow your gum. So, if you swallow your gum, no one will die."

"That's ridiculous. Next you'll be saying that those beans I bought from that cow dealer the other day are really magical."

"Henry, we're at Chickenfeet. Everything here is magical."

"You see! I won't do it. I won't swallow my gum."

Despite hours of careful reasoning, screaming, crying, and even threats to show the picture of him at two years old and diaperless around the school, Henry refused to swallow his gum. What Horrendous needed was someone who was an expert at sneaky planning, sabotage, and coercion. Since the only people like that were the teachers, Horrendous reluctantly recruited Really Wimpy to help her.

All that night, the Heroes' dorm bustled with the sounds of footsteps, muffled dirty words, and the screeches of trodden-upon cats as Horrendous and Really snuck up and down the stairs without making a single noise. Their arms were laden with a heavy mirror, Gizzard's Professional Official Dictionary, and Really Wimpy's purple makeup kit.

When Henry woke up, he pulled his gum off the bedpost and gave it a few stomps with his shoe to soften it up, then popped it in his mouth. He stumbled sleepily to the mirror on the opposite wall, blinking hazily at the images of mmmms, the candy that melts all over your hands and makes you look dumb.

He fiddled with the knob for a moment, until the commercials faded, leaving an upside-down image that pantomimed dirty words at him and had all the freckles reversed. But today something was different!

At first, he couldn't tell what. Then, at last, the realization came to Henry in a brilliant flicker of knowledge, about half the brightness of a dead firefly. His image had the mysterious words "gum your swallow" tattooed on his forehead in hot pink lipstick.

"What does it say?" he asked his mirror image, all four of their eyes popping open like shaken up sodas at this new revelation. Perhaps it was the clue that would solve all the mysteries of the book. Or better yet, it could be the final answer on the gameshow, *Who Wants To Be a Smartypants*? He knew the image was smarter than he was, since it always had his homework in its pocket just like Henry did. But the mirror's homework was done in a secret, unreadable code.

"Can't tell you that. You'll have to figure it out for yourself."

"Oh," Henry said.

He sat down and he thought.

And he thought.

And he thought.

And he thought.

And he thought.

And he thought.

And he thought.

And he thought.

And he thought.

And he thought.

And he thought.

And he thought.

And he thought.

And he thought.

"Any more of this and the readers will put the book down," Henry complained.

"Oh, all right. It says…" the mirror paused mysteriously to let the silence heighten everyone's expectations. "Gum your swallow."

"I know that!" Henry said. "I mean, what does it mean?"

"It's telling you to swallow your gum. I guess someone wrote it backwards to make it more mysterious."

"I see," Henry said. Well, if the mirror said to…he gulped and swallowed his gum.

"Yes!" Horrendous raced into the room with a huge grin, waving a flag that said "I won, I won and you didn't, nyah nyah nyah."

"We won. Now that you've swallowed your gum, no one will die!"

Lord Revolting watched them in his crystal ball and laughed and laughed and laughed.

The feather duster he stood on was tickling his feet.

Henry approached his dorm with trepidation. Three days had passed in a manner so ordinary and uneventful that they'd been completely left out of the book. He had a nasty suspicion that his peaceful days were over, and he'd enter his dorm to find something disgusting and horrible. Besides, the faint noises reminiscent of a giant rubber boot squelching through decaying banana peels were tipping him off.

"Password?" the fat lady portrait asked.

"I have a little vacuum, I made it out of clay. When I tried to fly on it, it broke, what can I say?"

"Now do the little dance," the painting prompted.

Henry sighed. The things he did just to enter his own room. At least the password featuring Irish step dancing and drums had expired.

Henry entered the dorm room to find Really Wimpy sniffling into his bed sheets. Apparently, he'd made those truly horrible noises by blowing his nose.

"Really, you're crying! What is it?"

"Crying? It's when your nose runs and your eyes feel they have to keep up."

"No, what's wrong?"

"It's just...well, I don't know quite how to say it. It's so horrible..."

"The cafeteria's serving vulture liver again this week?"

Really shook his head, sniffling loudly.

"No! They didn't find their pumpkin-fried toad recipe?"

"Worse. My pet rock's run away!"

Chapter 6:

THE RUNAWAY ROCK

After the shock wore off, it only took a short time to break into search parties. After what had happened to his goldfish, Henry was determined to never let a pet fall into Lord Revolting's hands again. A rock might be unflushable, but that wouldn't save it from such fates as a paperweight or, heavens forbid, a doorstop! They had to find that rock again.

Henry noticed Really Wimpy still sniffling as he set a mousetrap, baiting it with sand. "That's your best idea?"

Really was sniffling too loudly to hear him.

"Hey!" Henry said. "Maybe we should play some music to make Flaky shift closer."

"Like what?"

"Rock and Roll!"

Unfortunately, like most of Henry's brilliant ideas, the music trap failed to work. A team of students trained in following footprints eventually managed to track the rock to its hiding place. Somehow it had inserted itself behind a swarm of magical traps, designed to stop the foolish, the cowardly, and the incompetent. The problem was, this meant no one at Chickenfeet was qualified to recover it.

"All right," Really Wimpy told all of his friends and fellow students. "I'm leading an expedition past the basement's magical traps and maze of deadly doors to find my rock. And I need some volunteers." He turned away for a moment to check behind him for enemy rock kidnappers, or perhaps a teacher who would yell at them all for skipping class. The students exchanged surprised glances, amazed by Really Wimpy's determination. In truth, Really Wimpy could be quite courageous when something important was at stake, especially since he wasn't planning on going with the expedition.

Upon Really's call for volunteers, everyone took a step back except for Henry, who was taxing all his brain power trying to figure out why toucans had that name if there was only one of them.

Really turned back and grinned. "Henry, old pal! I should've known you'd brave all sorts of magical dangers that could savagely rip you in half and burn you to a crisp just so you could rescue my pet rock!"

"Er, well—" Henry started to say.

"And I'm sure that you can pass the dozens of *intellectual traps.*" Really glanced towards Horrendous where she stood with all of the sensible non-suicidal students.

Horrendous scowled. "All right, all right, I'll come. No one's facing any sort of test without me along."

"Great," Really Wimpy said. "I now have a fearsome team to attempt Mission Operation: Recover Our Nice Stone. Or for short, MORONS."

"Yes!" said Henry, who was starting to get into the spirit of things now that he knew Horrendous was going. She was tall enough to hide behind if any sort of crisis came up. "Let's hear it for the MORONS! Gimme an M, gimme an O, gimme an N, gimme an O, gimme an R, gimme an S! What's that spell?"

"Monors," Really Wimpy and Horrendous chorused.

Horrendous sighed. "You both should know, this plan sounds preposterous and imbecilic. It doesn't stand a chance of working."

"Great, all my trademarks," Henry said. "That's why people look up to me. 'Cause I do things the heroic way."

"I can see the two of you need me along after all."

"Absolutely," Henry said, not wanting his shield to escape and leave him alone with Really Wimpy. Granted, the two boys could try hiding behind each other, but somehow Henry had the feeling that that wouldn't work out properly.

"Are we really going up against the traps the teachers made?"

Really asked. "Bumbling Bore and Miss McGonk have intellects that we could only dream of."

"Hey, we can handle this," Henry said. "I just started using a new tooth whitener, guaranteed to produce that extra heroic grin."

"I think, in Henry's case, a can of dog food has an intellect that he can only dream of," Horrendous said.

Henry struck a macho pose, and turned to the few students who hadn't left to find something more entertaining to do, such as watching the Adventures of Wassie, the loyal gizzard's rabbit, who always wiggled her ears when someone was in danger. "If we're not back in ten minutes," Henry said, and paused dramatically while trying to figure out how to end his sentence. "Wait longer," he finally finished, a bit deflated.

"Hey," Really Wimpy said. "If you guys die in there, can I have your *The Noble History of Quick-Grab-the-Fish and How to Cheat Your Teammates*?"

"What do you mean?" Horrendous asked. "You're coming along."

"Wait!" Henry said.

"What now?" Horrendous asked.

"We need to assign jobs."

"You mean like, garbage collector and fireman and so forth?" Really Wimpy asked.

"No, he means jobs in the group," Horrendous said. "So, who's going to be the leader?"

"You're kidding, right?" Henry asked. "As the hero of the story, that's my job." He drew himself up in an imposing pose.

"So you don't have a problem standing in front, being the first one to encounter all the danger?" Horrendous asked.

"Er...Horrendous, I feel that we should share the group responsibility, in the interests of gender equality and fairness. Let's say I'll take the decision making and you take the part about standing in front, all right?"

After suffering through the tormenting agony of several ick-kay ou-yay in-way e-thay ehind-bay ith-way a-way oot-bay spells, Henry decided that assigning Horrendous the job of decoy wouldn't be taking full advantage of all her talents. So, before they set out on their expedition, he assigned her the further jobs of covering everyone's escape and standing in the way of anything dangerous before it could hurt the chief leader. Of course, giving Really Wimpy an assignment other than being the first to retreat would've been a waste of time.

As the official leader, Henry's first order was that his two followers both spend the next few minutes making him an enormous pile of macaroni dragons with cheese and canned ravioli. After all, he had no wish to go hungry while searching for immediate death. After his friends had left, he said to nothing in particular, "Hey, conscience, which way do I go to get the rock back?"

Sparkling gold words (except here and there where the glitter was flaking off to reveal smudgy green plastic words) appeared in midair. "I'm sorry, I'm not available right now, since I'm off to my annual retreat for consciences: Make them be all they can be, while you sit back and read the comics. Please leave a message after the blip. Blip."

"What! How could you abandon me like this? Right when I actually need you?" Apparently his conscience was only useful for helping him to dodge school rules, cheat at classes, and outwit Mr. Filth. Not that the last one was very hard.

A soft voice echoed through the corridor. "There comes a time, my son, when all mentors must step back and allow their students to mess up all on their own. It was written into our contracts at the dawn of time."

"Well, that's dumb." Henry considered. "If you're not there, how am I speaking to you?"

"I am with you. I will always be with you. For you see, I am inside you. I am in your heart and your soul and three of my toes are lodged in your left kidney."

Anything else the conscience said was drowned out in the noises of Henry's frantic hacking and gagging as he struggled to cough up several organs.

When Henry's friends returned, he proposed that they spy on the teachers. "Maybe one of them will casually drop hints about how to solve the traps without getting killed!"

They spent several minutes hiding in the trash bin outside Bumbling Bore's office, while the principal fed Socks her daily diet of birdseed, coffee, sarm bars, and double-caffeine-cola, to keep Socks awake while she shared a room with the professor. Finally, the children heard him say, "I hope I remember next time I go into the Maze of Traps to hop on one foot and whistle, since that will make the dangers disappear."

Unfortunately, the children left too quickly to hear Bumbling Bore mutter, "That'll show the little brats, won't it, Socks?" Socks squawked and nibbled sympathetically on the headmaster's toupee, undetectably poking a hole for the light to glint off Bumbling Bore's bald spot.

The three children approached the door to the maze of traps, marked "Caution: Secret Area. Do Not Notice. In Fact, Do Not Read This Sign At All."

"Oh dear," Horrendous said. "Well, maybe we won't get in. They've certainly locked the place."

"Yes, we will!" Henry said. "We can do whatever we set out to. Even create a nonfat ice cream that actually tastes good!" He noticed that his friends were looking at him oddly. "Well, let's begin with the door, all right?"

Really Wimpy pounded on the door. "It won't open! We're doomed, we're all doomed." And he began to cry.

"Stop it," Horrendous said, stepping over Really's flailing body. "We just need the proper password. Um, Open, door!" Nothing happened.

Henry attempted the hopping and whistling that his teacher had mentioned, but only succeeded in making a total fool of himself. At last he stopped. "Have I been making a total fool of myself?"

"Yes, you've been making a total fool of yourself," his friends called, as Horrendous left off her calculations and Really left off his crying long enough to belittle their leader by laughing and pointing.

"Open Sesame Seeds," Horrendous tried. Nothing.

"Open Sesame Seeds on a Toasted Bun With a Hamburger!" Horrendous yelled in desperation. The door refused to budge.

"Come on, Horrendous, use your head!" Henry commanded.

Horrendous gave him a glare fiery enough to barbeque him where he stood. "I'd rather use yours," she said, and shoved him into the door headfirst. Henry's head struck the latch and the door opened obediently.

"Hmm, fancy that. It was unlocked all this time," Horrendous said, walking through and leaving Henry stunned in the doorway.

The dark, spooky corridor sent chills up their spines, thanks to someone's leaving the air conditioning going full blast. Paper bats fluttered from cheap yarn, giving the impression of a haunted house designed by six-year-olds. The spooky sound effects tape wouldn't have frightened a paranoid mouse. Upon hearing it, Really Wimpy yelped and dove behind Horrendous. A table labeled "gizzard body parts" held bowls of peeled grapes, cold spaghetti, and ogre nostrils (Chickenfeet new age gizzards are very attached to their nostrils, after all. Their brains are in much lower demand).

"Stop!" Henry shouted from the doorway.

"What? You want to go first?" Really Wimpy asked.

"No. I want you leave your money and chocolate bars here with me. For, um, safe keeping."

"Stop that and get up," Horrendous said. "You know the book focuses on you, and you wouldn't want to leave the readers sitting in the corridor with you instead of following the adventure!"

"Oh, all right," Henry said and dragged himself to his feet. "I guess you have a point." He wandered into the room. "Wow, refreshments!" he said, and quickly scarfed down the ogre nostrils.

Meanwhile, Really Wimpy noticed a manhole in the center of the floor. "Look!" he said, dramatically pointing. "A manhole!"

"Yes it is!" Horrendous said.

"Wow, look, a manhole!" said Henry, who'd been chomping on cold spaghetti instead of paying attention. He set down his backpack full of emergency food and clean underwear so he could grab the gizzard's liver (actually a horse liver) in his other hand.

The sign on the manhole said, "Students shouldn't be close enough to read this. But if they've broken through the first door, I doubt my sign's going to keep them from breaking through this one. They just better not."

Horrendous looked at Henry and raised her eyebrows.

"What?"

"Shouldn't you give a speech about how we have to break as many school rules as possible, then jump into the hole without even checking what's down there?"

Henry paused in his search for more eatables to consider her suggestion for a few milliseconds. "No, that really sounds more like your type of thing, Horrendous. You can go first."

"Really Wimpy," Horrendous said sweetly. "It sounds as if our *dear* friend Henry needs us to support him and back his heroic deeds."

"Right!" Really said. Together they picked Henry up and heaved him into the manhole.

A moment passed. "Henry? Still alive?" Really called plaintively. If he had died, they would get to go home.

"Hey, check it out, it's totally groovy down here," Henry's voice called, as if from a long distance. In actuality, he was talking through a paper towel tube that he had brought in case he should feel the need for impressive acoustics.

Really stepped close to the edge, and held his nose tightly. "Cannonball!" he shouted, diving into the pit below. A moment later, he called out to Horrendous, "Come on down, it's not too bad! Something soft and squashy broke my fall. Lucky it was here."

Then she heard a muffled voice shout, "Get off me, or no autographed Henry Potty toothbrush!" Horrendous smiled, pinched her nose as well, and dived in. Maybe this would be more fun than she'd thought.

They spent three entire pages of the book arguing, blaming each other, and getting untangled, but made a unanimous motion to cut those pages and get to the good stuff.

"Look, Chapter Seven's coming up!" Horrendous said. They were surrounded by darkness so incredibly dark that there was no need to describe the scenery. "Henry, you'd better get the box."

"What box?"

"The box that the Star Gazer gave you."

"How did you know about that? I was invisible."

"I was perfecting my x-ray vision spell. Professor Bumbling Bore asked me to make one for extra credit and give him the recipe. I think he said something about a soccer room."

She stared at him pointedly. Always happy to return a favor, especially if it didn't cost any effort or money, Henry stared back at her. Horrendous tapped her toe. Henry stared at it, brow furrowing. "The box!" Horrendous prompted.

"Right, um, that box. Next time give me a hint, okay? I guess I left it by the peeled grapes."

"What! But we need it!" Horrendous screeched. Going on a quest with these two dimwits was starting to seriously get her goat. And one needs to hang onto all the goats one can get.

"Climb up and find it," Really Wimpy suggested.

Henry eyed the three story walls stretching vertically without a single handhold. They were running out of time. With every passing moment, Really's pet rock might crawl farther away. "Horrendous, do something!"

Horrendous paused, considered a moment, and wiggled her ears.

"Cool! I didn't know you could do that," Really Wimpy said.

"But how does that help us?" Henry asked.

"It doesn't. But you told me to do something. And I don't see any way of climbing back up there. As I see it, we have no choice but to go on."

Henry moved towards the single door leading out of their black, foul smelling chamber, muttering things under his breath like, "what'd we bring a genius along for, anyway."

Electric lights surrounded the distant door, bestowing a sickly purple glow throughout the room. It read, "Danger. Students keep out of the secret, mysterious area, unless you want to be boiled to a pulp and spread on whole grain toast." Henry shivered. He couldn't stand whole grain toast. And the air conditioner was still pelting full blast.

A few minutes later, they passed a sign saying, "We really mean it." The next sign said, "We told you so." But before they reached that sign they would have to face…Stuffy.

Chapter 7:

STUFF AND DESTROYERS
AND DRAGONS,
OH MY!

Stuffy was a wooly mammoth, who fortunately didn't know he was extinct or he would have been in a great deal of trouble. He barred the corridor with his trunk while surreptitiously chewing his cud. "Tickets, please."

Henry eyed his badge, which read, "I'm Stuffleupupus, how may I help you?" Reddish brown and furry, he reminded Henry of a teddy bear who'd gone through too many wash cycles. He wasn't terribly threatening, but if he sat on Henry, the boy would be just as dead.

"Er, I'm sorry, I must've left mine at home," Henry said. "Would you mind just letting me pass very quickly; there's a good chum."

"Sorry, I can't do that if you haven't bought a ticket to see the secret area."

"Let us in!" Really Wimpy said.

"Not by the hair on my chinny-chin-chin," He waved his trunk like a crossing guard waves a hand for stay-put.

"Here, I'll tell you what," Henry suggested. "Why don't I take over here for you? You must be tired, you know, standing here all day long, waving your trunk about."

"Well, I would like to go see my friend, Big Burp," Stuffy confessed.

"Sure you would. Why don't I take these people's tickets while you go on and get a nice cup of peanut butter. Or whatever."

"Wow, thanks," Stuffy said. "Don't you want anything in return?"

"Nah, it's a pleasure to help you out." Henry kept his pasted on smile in place until the large creature had shambled off in search of his friend. "Chump," Henry muttered.

"Phew," Henry said as they left the room. "I thought it would be harder to slip past Higgle's pet."

"Um, Henry," Really Wimpy said. "I don't think that was Higgle's pet."

"Why not?"

"Because this one is!"

"Oh, look, it's a puppy," Horrendous said. "Isn't it adorable?"

"Actually, it's a rabbit," Henry said, glancing at the ordinary pink bunny. It seemed suspiciously innocent as it sat there, wiggling its nose. It was surrounded by carrots, lettuce, celery, and fruity kids' cereal, all perfectly normal rabbit fare. A basket of Easter eggs sat nearby, as well as some plant matter chewed beyond recognition with a little placard reading "Audrey III." Three doors led out of the room, two of them firmly shut. "When did you last have your eyes checked?"

"Checked?" Really Wimpy wondered. "Aren't her eyes solid brown?"

The rabbit flexed its ears and hopped towards them.

"Why did the bunny cross the road?" Henry asked, still trying to look in all directions at once for fear of a trap.

"To get to the other side," Really Wimpy said.

"Henry's right. Rabbits fear people. Why is this one coming closer?"

Within a moment, all their questions were answered. Breath stinking of fake lemon and raspberry, the rabbit stretched its mouth open very, very wide and swallowed them all in one surprising gulp.

"Where are we?" Henry asked. It was very, very, very, very dark. He considered doing a good deed to activate his good deed aura, but as he wandered along considering it, he tripped over something soft and heard a loud ow that sounded like Really Wimpy.

Horrendous said, "I think we just fell down a rabbit, whole."

"So, how do we get out?" Really Wimpy asked, climbing to his feet. He was not having a good day. Between losing his beloved pet rock, being forced to go on an adventure, meeting an extinct wooly mammoth more than twice his size, and being stepped on by Henry Potty, it was almost more than he could bear. Besides, it felt as if Henry had gum on his shoe.

"Bribe it with a ten carat ring," Horrendous said sarcastically.

"Great plan," Henry said, trying to be polite enough to activate his aura so he could see again. He didn't like tripping over Really Wimpy; it had felt like stepping on jello. Besides, it felt as if Really had gum in his hair. The good deed aura obediently brightened the place enough that they could see, and immediately Henry regretted summoning it.

They were inside a giant stomach.

(Aside: This may be obvious to the readers, since Henry and his friends were swallowed by the rabbit. In fact, it would be rather odd if the trio found themselves somewhere else, such as the sub-basement of the local video store, where they keep all the silent movies involving black and white little astronauts without space suits flying to the moon and walking around, with a rocket ship on an obvious string. However, this stomach was rather disgusting, being filled with pink, pulsing bits, and puddles of stomach acid that sent nauseating scents drifting through the organ in question. Henry and his friends hadn't realized the full repulsiveness of their situation until Henry's abuse of his conscience. Which just goes to show, that you should be conscientious about how you use the resources around you.

Also, to those who wonder how a tiny rabbit managed to swallow three nearly full-grown students, as well as their shoes, backpacks, and collections of rubber bands and erasers to be found in their pockets, the answer is simple. Unbeknownst to Henry and friends, or even Higgle, but knownst to the all-wise narrator, the legendary Midgard Serpent, a beast whose gullet encircles the world, had been turned into a harmless looking pink bunny the week before, as a birthday prank by his pals. When Higgle lured him into the tunnels below the school with a trail of rabbit treats, the Midgard serpent-now-rabbit went

69

along because he thought it would be better than sitting around doing his taxes. [Yes, even the Midgard Serpent does taxes. And when you consider how much space he takes up, and how much he consumes during the year, that comes down to a huge pile of forms.] And now, let us return to Henry and his companions, who have spent the entire past two paragraphs cooped up in an increasingly nauseating bunny stomach, having fallen down a rabbit, whole.)

"Well, finally the story returns to us," Horrendous muttered. "You'd think we weren't important or something."

"We all know I'm important," Henry announced. "I'm—"

"We know, we know," Horrendous and Really chorused.

"Time's running out!" Really said. "Terrible peril surrounds my poor rock!"

Horrendous patted him on the shoulder. "We'll arrive just at the last instant. That's how it always works in these stories."

"Yeah, I guess you're right." Really brightened. "That makes me the brainy sidekick, right?"

Horrendous quickly searched for a distraction. "Henry? Any ideas?"

"Just one. It's risky and dangerous but I'm willing to try." Henry started hopping on one foot and whistling continuously, until he slipped with his supporting foot and ended up face down in a pile of stomach sludge. Really and Horrendous grinned in relief. At least the horrible, air-shattering noise had ceased.

"The question is, why did the rabbit eat us?" Horrendous said. "It isn't like we're carrying carrots, or colorful tooth-rotting cereal, or anything rabbits would want." Then she gasped. A moment later she gasped again. Then she gasped yet a third time.

"What is it? Have you found the answer?" Really Wimpy asked.

"No, I think I'm just allergic to rabbit interiors."

"Hey, look!" Really Wimpy noticed something silvery shining in the puddles of goo dotting the rabbit's belly. "Henry must've dropped it."

Horrendous picked up the silvery object. "Well, this explains why the rabbit wanted us," she muttered. From outside the rabbit, the sounds of deep, rhythmic drumming could be heard. Really glanced around the stomach, trembling with his usual terror, and then his eyes returned inevitably to the object in Horrendous's hand. It was a twin pack of batteries.

"So how do we get out of here?" Really asked.

From his puddle of sludge, Henry mumbled something heroic and useless, such as "we need a plan!" His two friends ignored him.

"Why don't we tickle the inside of the stomach," Horrendous suggested at last. "Maybe the beast will vomit us up!"

Her suggestion was greeted with boyish cries of "Oh gross, hey, let's do it!" from both of her rabbit-stomach-mates and the plan was complete.

There was only one problem. This rabbit didn't seem to have a ticklish or even overly sensitive stomach lining. The three inept gizzards spent hours poking, prodding, and reenacting "this little piggy went to market." Nothing.

"So now what?" Henry asked as they slumped in the stomach acid, exhausted from the hours of tickling and cajoling.

There was silence throughout the stomach chamber. Henry tried again. "Horrendous? Now what?"

"I don't know."

"What!" both boys asked, shaken to their cores. Horrendous's announcement was the most startling thing they'd heard all day, and considering the kind of day they were having, that said a great deal.

"Well, you can't expect me to have all the answers, all the time!" The boys continued to stare at her in patent disbelief. "All right, all right," Horrendous conceded. "I guess I have another solution. Does anyone have a can of prunes?"

(The following section has been deemed far too disgusting for any normal reader to experience. Therefore it has been cut, in the interests of readers not experiencing it. The author will only supply a few, necessary details: 1. All three students managed to escape from the rabbit. 2. Higgle's bunny, also known as The Destroyer, was feeling rather unwell, and therefore went home to have a cup of hot carrot soup and a nap. 3. The children found themselves rather desperately wanting showers. Unfortunately, all they had was a single package of ready-wipes from Horrendous's purse, which vanished rather quickly, considering that three of them needed to clean up. 4. The thought penetrated Stuffy's peanut-sized brain that someone might have somehow managed to slip by him. So he sat down at his guard post to ponder this, effectively blocking the exit and incidentally, the route to the showers. Author's note ends.)

The three disgusting students exchanged glances. "The rock's peril ever increases," Henry exclaimed. "Only we can save it from a fate worse than paperweights. Well, no way to go but forwards!" He took two steps, and then slipped in an extra pile of rabbit muck that no one had noticed. He fell to the ground and began to involuntarily slide along it, butt forwards as he had said.

In fact, he slid straight through the open door number one, past the broken lock on the entrance with an "out of order" sticker. A horrified cry burst from the room. Horrendous tried to exchange an exasperated glance with Really Wimpy, but discovered that he was cowering behind her back. With a sigh, she strode forwards on her own. After all, Henry owed her quite a bit of cash for all the homework she'd finished for him. Dragging Really along behind her, Horrendous yanked open the door, determined to find out what had frightened Henry enough to make him scream. With any luck, it would be nothing more than a tuna sandwich.

It was a dragon.

More precisely, it was a drag-on.

Dragons are ferocious monsters, vaguely reptilian, whose favorite meal is knight-on-a-bun. Drag-ons, on the other hand, are far more dangerous, scary, and all around vicious. They are the history teachers who drone on for hours upon end without reaching a point, the door-to-door salesmen who can't stop selling, the politicians and school principals who babble for hours while people just want to get to the cookies and punch at the back of the room.

"This isn't the way you should be going," the drag-on remarked. He was a short, stumpy little man with a frizzy mustache and a stained tie. His red plaid jacket and blue pants didn't match his brown shoes. "I think that you should turn back and go right around back the way you came. After all, where we come from is very important. In fact, I'm from a little town called Weeping Water. Not that the water actually cried or anything. That's just what the town was called. I remember a time when it rained for three days straight and I thought…"

Horrendous's eyes drifted closed. "You fiend," she muttered as her voice slurred to a snore.

"Run!" Really Wimpy shouted. "He's trying to turn our brains to jelly."

Henry shrugged from where he still sat on the floor. "I don't feel anything odd."

Horrendous, who had far too many brains to want to lose them, roused herself and grabbed one of Henry's arms. Really Wimpy, who had just enough brains to copy what Horrendous did, grabbed his other arm and pulled as well. This would've been a far more effective technique if they'd both been tugging in the same direction.

"No, stop pulling. Ow!" Henry yelled. "I'll give you each a pair of Henry Potty exclusive limited offer boxer shorts if you'll let me go!"

Untempted by the boxer shorts, his friends kept pulling. However, Really and Horrendous managed to coordinate their efforts to tug the same way before their friendship with Henry, not to mention Henry himself, was torn apart.

They rushed back to relative safety and were careful to choose door number two instead of door number one. It opened into darkness.

"Wait!" Really said. "We can't go in there. The light's out!"

Henry gazed thoughtfully at the tall, iron lamppost. "Perhaps this isn't a lantern, but a beacon, shining the way to an astounding world of magic, with fawns, lions, and even properly spelled witches!"

The lamppost flared into brilliance and Henry crowed with delight. "You see! This is the gateway to a magical world of untold wonders! Maybe they'll make me their high king. We can forget Lord Revolting and embark on a magical adventure to unknown lands!"

"'Fraid not," Horrendous called. "Someone just forgot to flip the switch." She moved away from the light switch she'd just turned on. "Now let's go see what this maze will throw at us next." She turned her head at luckily the right moment to avoid the first tennis ball that plummeted from the ceiling, but she wasn't lucky enough to dodge the three hundred more or so that followed.

☆ ☆ ☆

"Wow," Really Wimpy said, when the tennis balls had finished their plummeting. "Stuffy, the Battery Bunny, and then a drag-on. I hope that's enough weird gatekeepers for a while."

"Oh, no. It's another one!" Henry said, staring straight ahead. "A short, ugly guy with uncombed hair and ears that stick out. How will we get past him?"

"We don't have to," Horrendous said dryly. "It's a mirror."

A tall, shiny mirror hung prominently on a door, just as Horrendous had commented in the previous paragraph. Its mesmerizing purple frame glittered with chartreuse stars. Unfortunately, there was no handle or other method to open the door. Now that she had turned the lamppost on, the children could see that there was nothing interesting in the room except for a vending machine, and they were all out of quarters.

"Quick!" Henry said. "Let's analyze the name of the mirror. Maybe if we spell it backward, or jumble the letters up in a hat, or erase all the words and rewrite them with better handwriting, it'll give us a clue!"

"Henry, that's a great idea," Horrendous said. "There's just one tiny little snag."

"What's that?"

"This mirror doesn't have a name on it."

"Maybe we have to ask." Really Wimpy approached it shyly. "Mirror, mirror on the wall," he started.

"Oh, be quiet," the mirror said. Its voice was friendly and animated as a talk show host on daytime TV. While it spoke, the mirror's surface projected little illustrations to accompany its words, seamlessly blending badly-drawn stick figures with bubby cartoons. "I get enough of that already. Just tell me what you want."

Henry stepped forwards and struck a bold, dramatic pose. "We wish to pass! Whatever the danger, whatever the obstacle, I will conquer it. For I am the hero!"

"Very well. This is a challenge of intelligence."

Henry hastily stepped back. "Horrendous, maybe I'll let you tackle this one."

Horrendous eagerly took Henry's place. "Ask away."

"There are three questions before you may pass. What is your quest?"

"To defeat Lord Revolting so Henry can have revenge for his goldfish, and give him such a humiliatingly big wedgie that he never comes back."

"That is correct. If the earth spins at a rate of K, and you have a tunafish sandwich for lunch, while John wears an orange shirt, how old is Fanny's pet turtle?"

Horrendous studied the question, knitting her brow, and then slowly unraveling it. "Eight!"

"That is correct."

Henry gaped. "How'd you know that?"

Horrendous shrugged. "It's obvious."

"If George Washington went to Washington state while Mrs. Washington stayed behind to wash Washington's woolies and wring them dry, how many w's are there in all?"

"Eight!" Horrendous said again.

"Sorry, there are no w's in the word 'all.'"

A trapdoor opened under Horrendous's feet and she plummeted through, shrieking.

"It got Horrendous!" Really hollered.

"On Saturday at noon we should have ten minutes of reciting useless facts as a mark of respect," Henry said. He bowed his head for a moment. "Now let's get that pet rock."

"What about Horrendous?"

"She knew the risks. Now that she's gone, it's our duty to abandon her in order to reach the end of the book. She'd want us to."

"Wouldn't she want us to help her?"

"If we don't find that rock we won't be heroes, we'll just be two students breaking school rules for no apparent reason. I doubt they'd even cancel our punishments, let alone give us a big party. Now, let's go." Henry started towards the door.

"Wait!" the mirror said. "There's one more question for you to answer. I need three right answers before anyone passes."

"Okay, what is it?" Henry asked, trying to control the screams of terror that he felt bubbling up deep inside him. Or perhaps it was the canned ravioli.

"What is 5 plus 3?"

75

"Um, I'm not really sure. Horrendous always used to do this sort of thing for me. Can you give me a hint?"

"It's the same as four and four."

"Oh, gee. If only I had four fingers on each hand, like that cartoon family. Then I could figure this out. Um…" Henry stared at all of his fingers and finally pulled off socks and shoes to add toes to his calculations. At last, he had a reasonable answer, made up of careful deduction and equations. "Forty-seven."

"That's not even close," the mirror said. Bursts of flame exploded from three of the chartreuse stars in a cacophony of heat, noise, and those little burn marks that never wash off. Before he had time to think, Henry died.

Chapter 8:

TO BE KICKED OUT OR
NOT TO BE

W hat!" Henry Potty shouted. "I'm not supposed to die! I'm the main character. My name's in the title. I'm essential to this book." He was standing disconcertingly next to the book, instead of in it where he belonged. His tiny feet wobbled on the AUTHOR'S desk and a bright lamp shone into his face, fading the rest of the room into darkness. Judging by the gigantic size of the AUTHOR in her chair, Henry decided that he was about four inches tall.

The AUTHOR shrugged and flicked Henry onto his posterior with her pencil's eraser end. "I thought it'd be unexpected. Readers want surprises."

"Put me back! You can't kill me."

"I just did. And now, if you don't mind, I have a story to finish."

"How?" Henry demanded. "How will you end it without me?"

"Very simple. Higgle will find the rock when he enters the Maze of Traps through the back door to do his spring cleaning. He'll give it to Really Wimpy, who will realize that he doesn't need the rock after all, since he has real friends. If he taps the rock on the ground three times, it'll take him back to the farm in Kansas where he grew up. There he can live a happy life with all his pals. Except you, Henry, because you're dead."

"That's the dumbest thing I ever heard of," Henry said.

The AUTHOR shrugged. "It's worked before."

"Fix the story and make me live. I want to save the day."

"Now why should I do that?"

"Without Henry Potty, Chickenfeet is just a pathetic school where students get bad grades, teachers bore students, and everyone skips classes to find a pet rock. It's just a background for my heroism. With Henry Potty, Chickenfeet is…" Henry's voice trailed off.

"Yes?"

"That is, sometimes I…"

"Do continue," the AUTHOR prompted, after Henry's silence had dragged on for nearly twenty minutes.

"People need me to…"

The AUTHOR lifted her eraser and moved it closer to Henry. "The book needs a hero," he squeaked. "Someone to make vague threatening statements at the bad guy. A champion to prove that good can win in the end, even through total stupidity and simple luck. Someone to show the world that BEING BRAINLESS AND COURAGEOUS IN A PIG-HEADED WAY IS SOMETHING WE CAN ALL ASPIRE TO!!!"

The AUTHOR considered that for a moment. "You're right," she said. Henry slumped with relief. "But Really Wimpy can fill that role equally well." The Author moved the eraser down in one decisive movement.

"No!" Henry shrieked, diving out of the way. He shoved at the book beside him, pushing it close to the wastepaper bin. "Write me back in or I'll dump it!"

The AUTHOR sighed. "The first person to say this book belongs in a trash bin. You think they're your friends, but they always turn on you. All right, all right," she added as Henry gave it another shove. "I'll write you back in. Just give me a moment…" She picked Henry up by the scruff of his neck and disgustedly dropped him back into the story.

"Forty-seven."

"That's not even close," the mirror said. Bursts of flame exploded from three of the chartreuse stars in a cacophony of heat, noise, and those little burn marks that never wash off. Before he had time to think, Henry…

"You said you'd let me live!"

"I am. Stop whining."

Before he had time to think, Henry snatched a rock that fell from the sky and hit him on the head. A little tag on it read "From a mysterious, secret, unnamed friend. Not the same one as earlier."

"Wow," Henry muttered. "Great timing." He hurled the rock into the mirror with all his might. The mirror exploded with an enormous crash, showering the two boys with needles of glass. As they shrieked, the door popped open, revealing yet another plain hallway. This one was partially unfinished. A ladder and three buckets of paint revealed that someone had been busy painting over the floral wallpaper in the same dull beige of the previous corridors.

"Well, at least my luck's starting to change." Henry stepped over the broken mirror fragments, rubbing the substantial bump on his head. "A mysterious friend gave me the rock, and I cheated the test of intelligence. Things can't get better." He strode through the shattered glass, ignoring the black cat that raced across his path. Then Henry ducked under the ladder draped across the hallway and kept walking, with Really Wimpy stumbling nervously behind. They walked down the long, straight, narrow hallway, until they reached what they hoped would be the last door.

"Um, Henry?"

"Yes," Henry replied in his most heroic voice. "What is it, true friend and dearest companion?"

Really Wimpy blushed and whispered something in Henry's ear. A short murmured conversation followed, with exclamations of "can't it wait?" and "why didn't you go before you left?" In the end, the quest paused for an hour or two while Henry and Wimpy hiked back to the beginning of their journey in search of an elusive little gizzard's room. At last they returned to their previous location before the mysterious door.

A small placard mounted on it said "End of the Road." This door was actually locked.

"So how're we going to get through?" Really Wimpy asked, fingering his lucky whistle that always served to keep him out of jams. If he sat still and blew it long enough, someone always came to save him. Then the rescuer would yell at him for wasting time, but at least Really would technically be rescued.

"I know!" Henry said. "We can build a giant wooden statue of Lord Revolting, and when someone opens the gate and takes the statue inside, we can leap out and attack!"

"Will that really work?"

"Of course, it's a classic strategy, dating all the way back to the cult movies of the 1970's."

"Oh. How do we know there's anyone on the other side?" Really Wimpy asked.

"Always criticizing! Next you'll think we should check the place for mines before beginning construction."

Really Wimpy glanced around at the pits and blackened craters in the floor and decided not to comment. He would just station himself near the exit and stay ready to bolt. "What will we build the statue out of?"

Henry shrugged. "You know, stuff," he said vaguely. "Anything that's lying around."

"There's nothing here except blackened craters and parrot feathers. Plus that old bucket and mop in the corner."

"Then that's what we'll use."

Really Wimpy flinched. He wasn't sure he wanted his pet rock this badly, not if it involved the slightest bit of effort, let alone physical danger. Besides, he was allergic to parrot feathers.

The disguise was very impressive. It wasn't exactly a giant, hollow statue, Henry explained, since that would involve actual building materials. Still, they had done the best they could. Both of the boys were smeared from head to foot with soot from the craters. They wove festoons of colorful parrot feathers into their hair, and stuck them to their bodies with the tube of superglue that Henry had luckily kept in his pocket after gluing Miffie's braids to her desk a few days before. Henry wore the bucket on his head as a sort of helmet, while Really Wimpy was left with the mop.

Really Wimpy's role as brainy sidekick hadn't prepared him to do such reckless and idiotic things. "So now they'll think we're a statue and let us in?" he asked, sniffling as much from the parrot feathers as his own inherently wimpy nature.

"Exactly," Henry said, pushing back his bucket helmet.

"And then when night falls, we climb out of ourselves?"

"Something like that. Don't bother me with details; we should just take this one step at a time." Henry took one step forward, trod on a blob of spilled superglue, and was immediately stuck to the floor. He glanced at his foot. "Maybe this wasn't the right step," he said weakly.

He discarded his neon green air pump tennis shoe (at least it was the left one) and continued forward, Really Wimpy proudly cowering at his back.

They stood outside the door for a while, waiting for someone to decide that they were statues and carry them inside.

"Henry?" Really Wimpy whispered through gritted teeth.

"Oh, no, not again. We don't have time for all these pit stops."

"No, it's something else."

"Quiet," Henry whispered back. "We're supposed to be statues."

There was a pause, and then Really whispered again. "Could we try that door knocker?"

"What door knocker?"

"The one on the door."

"Oh, that door knocker."

Henry knocked. A small peephole opened and a green eye glared down at them. "We don't want any."

"Have you seen a pet rock wandering around?" Really Wimpy asked pathetically.

"Get lost," the doorkeeper said. And he slammed the peephole in their faces.

Really sat down on the steps and promptly started crying very loudly.

"Really, hush!" Henry said. "You're embarrassing me!" Really just kept sobbing. After a few moments, the door in front of them opened. Really stood up. "Yes! I knew it would work."

"Really, you got the door open! How?"

Really Wimpy shrugged modestly. "I read it in *The Wizard of Oz*." He triumphantly entered the room, with Henry behind him.

☆ ☆ ☆

"Not so fast," the gatekeeper said with a throaty growl. His hulking body folded uneasily into his desk chair, which seemed at least two sizes too small. He sat behind his desk, keeping watch over the red and white striped tollgate. A large stop sign rested close to his meaty hand, while a placard read, "exact change only, or we rearrange your face." He looked like a hairless troll, only more menacing. "I may have a soft spot for tears, but you still have to pay the toll. It's going to cost you your left foot to enter."

"What?" Henry asked. He wasn't the type of hero to make heroic sacrifices.

"By the way, are you students?"

"Yes," Really Wimpy babbled, desperate to save his favorite foot. If he lost it, he wouldn't be able to chew those toenails any more. "Absolutely, we're students, yes."

"It'll only cost your left shoe with a student card."

Really Wimpy gratefully held out his card and moth-eaten brown sneaker.

"Thank you very much. In you go, then. Wait," he added before Henry could follow his friend. "You haven't given me your sneaker."

"Oh, right. It's glued to the floor back there, help yourself." Henry tried to slip past the doorman, but the tollgate remained firmly closed.

"I'm sorry, but that's not good enough." The guard looked anything but sorry.

"Here, you can have my right shoe."

"No, that won't do either. Right shoes have too much wear and tear, no good friction left on the sole. I'll have to take your foot. Give me a moment to get the mini-guillotine."

Really Wimpy raced out of the room ahead, pet rock cradled lovingly in his arms. Socks the parrot flew furiously behind him, pecking at his hair and clawing at the back of his neck. Really Wimpy seemed oblivious to the parrot's mayhem. "Look, Henry! Flaky's back!"

"What happened?" Henry asked, quickly drawing his foot away before the guard at the gate could seize it. The guard gave a mild grunt of disappointment.

"I think Flaky and Socks fell in love. Isn't it terrific?"

"What?!"

"Yeah, it's amazing. When I went into the next room, I saw a whole nestful of petrified eggs."

Socks perched on the desk and muttered various insults about wimpy little boys who had to stick their noses in where they weren't wanted. Both boys ignored her.

"This's just strange. I mean, a bird and a rock? They can't be in love."

Really shrugged. "Apparently, even when one's not a bird, these two can."

"So we haven't been chasing after Lord Revolting after all?" Henry asked, feeling devastated. Or at least pathetic. How could he be the hero if he didn't defeat the bad guy? "I thought he needed a runaway rock to complete his spell of evil power."

"Yeah. What a surprise," Really said. "It was actually the least likely character in the book who lured Flaky down here. Who would have thought an ordinary gizzard's pet could be the bad guy?"

"I guess you have a point," Henry said. "But is the parrot really the least likely character to be the culprit?"

"No, I am!" the tollgate guard said from behind them. "I was the one who brought them down here. I thought with the famous Henry Potty busy searching, the fan t-shirts would disappear, and the market would be stagnant enough for me to sell my new, improved tollgate toothpaste. But it failed. And now I'm cast as the bad guy forever!" The tollgate guard put his head on his hands and burst into noisy sobs.

Really Wimpy blinked. "Well, that was random."

"Quick," Henry whispered. "Let's make tracks before he notices we're gone." And the two gizzards-in-training fled for their pet rock's life, leaving a bawling guard and a furious parrot behind them.

"I just wish I'd had a chance to fight Lord Revolting," Henry muttered as they puffed around the corner. They had nearly returned to the lamppost room. "I'd like to prove myself against powers far beyond my own."

"You could take an IQ test against one of Higgle's hot dogs," Really suggested.

Henry's eyes widened. "You!" he gasped, staring straight ahead. No one was there.

Chapter 9:

THE SECRET, UNEXPECTED
SURPRISE TWIST

U m, Henry, there's no one there," Really Wimpy said.
"I know, but I'm the hero. That means I should be dramatic
every chance I get."

Really shrugged. "If you say so. Oh, hi, Lord Revolting!"

Lord Revolting had indeed appeared in the corridor while Henry
and Really squabbled over the best way of being dramatic.

"Ah, my arch-nemesis, the disgusting Henry Potty. It seems your
luck's run out!"

Henry straightened in surprise, trying to make the best of his lost
dramatic moment. "Beam us up, Sputty!"

Unsurprisingly, nothing happened. It was Sputty's day off, after
all.

Henry felt for a sword, didn't have one, and found himself wishing
even more desperately for a can of air freshener. Lord Revolting's
stench sure hadn't improved. Henry raised his wand instead. "Fly, fly,
for we are lost!"

"I think you're supposed to fight him," Really Wimpy said in a
stage whisper, while Lord Revolting waited patiently.

"Oh." Henry tried a different tack. "Lord Revolting! What are *you*
doing here?"

Lord Revolting shrugged. "Trying to pretend you didn't know I'd show up now? You seem so interested in the pet rock that I decided I'd steal it from you. Because winning and taunting their opponents is what villains do best. Now give me the rock."

"When pigs fly!" Henry shouted. A winged pig soared overhead, ruining his line.

"Oh, come now, Henry. Let's be reasonable. You don't mind if I call you Henry, do you?"

"Well then, what do I call you?" Henry asked. His aura brightened at his politeness. He doubted he could actually hug the pile of rotting garbage before him, but it was a thought. Just not a very good one.

"None of your business," Lord Revolting growled.

"Oh, come on, your name can't be that bad," Henry coaxed. He had a nasty sign for the bathrooms all planned out.

"Oscar," Lord Revolting said. "But don't you dare tell anyone."

"Oscar? Your name's Oscar?" Henry and Really looked at each other for a moment, then burst into giggles.

"Stop it! It's not funny."

"Gee, Oscar, you sure are a grouch," Henry said.

As Lord Revolting snarled at the insult, Henry turned to Really Wimpy. "Quick, now's your chance! While I battle Lord Revolting, you can sneak off and leave me to hog the glory."

Really Wimpy was so amazed that he forgot to run away. "You're going to battle Lord Revolting yourself? A student versus the most powerful dark gizzard that's ever lived? How do you plan to do that?"

Henry shrugged. "I'll cheat, of course."

Lord Revolting interrupted their whispered conference by handing Henry a long list.

"What's this?"

"All the mysterious things I've been doing in the book and why I've done them. I thought it would save time."

"Oh. Thanks." Henry took the list and glanced over it quickly. He didn't bother sharing the list with the readers, since he planned to quiz Lord Revolting on everything on it, just to set the record straight. In the depths of his soul, Henry felt the injustice of having undergone a year of learning and exams, while Revolting hadn't had to attend a single class. Now, at last, he could take his revenge by beating Revolting in a climactic battle. One fact from the paper actually penetrated his beady brain. "You haven't been trying to live forever and be the most powerful evil gizzard in existence?" Henry asked. His head dropped into his hands as all his preconceived notions flitted away.

"Of course not," Lord Revolting said. "That's just what the author wanted you to think. My plan's far more appalling and sneaky than that. I've stolen all the homework of every child in this school and brought it down here. I was coincidentally just on the verge of destroying it when you walked in. Now I'm going to make it explode in a gigantic ball of flame, and you children will all have to stay here over summer vacation.

"No!!!!!!!!!!!!!!!" Henry shouted in horror. Then he realized that, while shouting in horror was all well and good, stopping Lord Revolting might also be a bright idea. Still, it was the hero's duty to have a long, detailed discussion with the bad guy before actually attacking him. "I should've noticed you were trying to destroy our summer vacation. It was totally obvious! I mean, all the clues were there. If you bought out Higgle's hot dog stand, you could out-compete our gourmet catsup-filled cafeteria lunches. And you were going to eat the magic mushrooms, grow to gigantic size, and squish our school! There must be a secret passage from the girls' bathroom to your magical underground lab."

"Actually, no, I was visiting the wicked witch who lives in the forest center. She's an old friend of mine, and bakes wonderful gingerbread. And my identical twin sister, Lady Moldy, was the one in the bathroom."

"But I didn't see her come out again. Did she steal my invisibility cloak? It disappeared last week."

"No, she just needed to stay in there a while after sampling your gourmet cafeteria food."

"And the hot dogs?"

Lord Revolting shrugged. "I really like magical hot dogs, that's all. But when I was in the post office, I sent the school administration a petition that I forced all your teachers to sign at wandpoint, demanding that your summer vacation be taken away. That's why I've been sneaking around your school for all this time."

Henry shook his head. "I can't see how I possibly missed that. All the clues were right in front of me." A sudden thought occurred to Henry, like the flash of a very, very dim bulb. "What about the unicorn blood? Don't tell me that was your identical twin sister."

"Oh no, you were right about my trying to live forever. Just a bit off on the evil gizzard thing. Don't worry; it could happen to anyone. And as it turns out, this unicorn and I didn't have compatible blood types. Now do you have any other questions? I'd be happy to stand around and answer them all before I kill you. I wouldn't want you to die while the readers are still confused."

"You want to live forever?"

Lord Revolting snorted, sounding rather like a diseased hippo. "Of course. How else could I discover the important things in life, like how many licks it takes to get to the center of a popsie roll toot?"

Henry stared at him, agog, aghast, horrified, and suddenly rather needing to skip out of the room and answer the call of nature himself. Darn Really Wimpy. "What? No one has the right to know the age-old popsie roll toot secret. You make me sick!"

"No, actually it's allergy season." Really Wimpy whispered from beside him. From behind his back, Really suddenly produced a pair of electric pink pom-poms that matched the writing on his sweater. "Are you going to fight him now? I'm all ready to back you up. Okay if I stand by the door in case you lose?"

Lord Revolting bared his teeth. "At last, the fight scene! Choose your weapon."

Henry considered his options. "Um, minigolf?"

Lord Revolting agreed with a snarl and they set off for the next room, which had a convenient eighteen holes all ready to go. At the seventh hole, Henry noticed that Revolting had been stacking the game by luring his golf ball around with a magnet. This act of foul cheating made every bone in Henry's body tremble with rage because he hadn't thought of it first. He'd only cheated with the scorecard, cleverly slipping unobtrusive ones in, transforming ones into elevens, and sevens into seventy-ones. Unfortunately, since this was golf, his score padding didn't help him a great deal.

Really Wimpy had just pointed this out (with Horrendous down in the subbasement, someone needed to stand in for her) when Henry caught Revolting cheating. This was the final straw! Actually, it was a convenient way out. Even if Henry had planned to suggest they switch to Hungry Hungry Harpies.

"So, foul heap of trash, you try to cheat me!" Henry proclaimed, throwing himself back into his heroic dramatics. "I don't know what idiot suggested we try this game, but I think it's time we fought a real fight!"

"You want to fight me?" Lord Revolting asked, drawing himself up to his full seven feet, seven inches and a half. Plus thick soled shoes.

"Um, yes," Henry's voice came out in a squeak. He quickly deepened it. "Yes, I want a fight."

Lord Revolting smiled. "As I expected. My Estroy-day Ermin-vay spell should be useful now. Not to mention the Mega-wedgie."

Henry smiled a confident, dangerous smile. It was the type of grin most commonly found on lunatics who believed that they could soar off of buildings and never hit the ground. "But I came prepared as well. I brought some...insurance." He held up a packet of papers and waved them menacingly. "And I also have a weapon. One no one could predict." He pulled a large, slimy, whole codfish from beneath his robe. Behind him he could hear Really Wimpy suck in his breath in an attempt to avoid the now doubly horrible smell.

Really Wimpy nervously tugged on Henry's sleeve. "Henry, how could you hide that under your robe so no one would notice? And for this long?"

"I'm the hero. I can do whatever I want. And it's my job to do the unexpected while living up to readers' expectations." Henry raised the cod over Revolting's head. As Lord Revolting cringed, Henry held the codfish over him, but didn't bring it down.

Really Wimpy stared at the cowering Lord Revolting. "Henry, you've got to kill him. He's the bad guy." Emotions warred over Henry's tormented face. Finally he dropped the giant codfish with a sigh of defeat

"I can't."

"But why not? Remember how he killed your goldfish!"

"I know that." Henry threw the cringing lord a look of pure disgust. "But he needs to return for the sequel."

Chapter 10:

DINOSAUR TIME

"What we need is a cruel and unusual punis hment," Really Wimpy said. "Something so terrifying and nasty that all sensible people have outlawed it, something that will put Lord Revolting in his place for good, until he escapes for the next book!"

Henry smiled evilly. "I know just the thing."

"But we're not allowed to play disco music at Chickenfeet."

"Not that."

"Another steak?" Really Wimpy asked. "Or a meatloaf? I don't think—"

Henry shook his head. "Not a steak. Something much, much worse."

He pointed his wand solemnly at Lord Revolting. "I'm sorry I have to do this. But Gillie must be revenged."

Really Wimpy tugged on his sleeve. "Don't you mean Goldie?"

"Whatever. Now your suffering begins! Expecta dinosaurus purplus."

Lord Revolting's face turned ashen. "No, no, not that, please! I'll do anything—"

Henry shook his head. "It's too late."

Happy singing drifted down the corridor, growing steadily louder. It sounded as though someone were chortling, "I love you…you love me…"

A dinosaurlike shadow loomed on the wall, and Lord Revolting fainted dead away.

☆ ☆ ☆

Horrendous rushed out of the lamppost room. "Henry! Are you all right?"

"Horrendous? How did you get out of there?"

She shrugged. "The book's nearly over, and I'm not supposed to die. So the mirror had to let me out. I can't believe I actually got an answer wrong!"

Henry turned towards her. "Hey, if you're such a know-it-all, then why do you have all those problems in classes?"

"I wrote eight thousand pages of homework, but they all disappeared somehow. I think someone up at the top definitely has it in for me. Gosh, I hate this school!" Just as she said those words, a grand piano plummeted out of the sky. Horrendous let out a single screech as it landed on her head.

"But I thought you wanted higher notes," Henry said. "Well, that's the breaks."

Horrendous could be heard murmuring the words to the oilet-tay on-way our-yay ead-hay and iano-pay up-way our-yay ear-ray end-way spells from under the grand piano as Henry walked back towards the academy, blissfully unaware of his upcoming fate.

Henry strode proudly out the front door of Chickenfeet, shaking toilet water from his hair and moving with a curious, lurching gait. His arms were laden with rotten fruit, forcefully thrown gifts from all his friends and classmates in revenge for his inviting the purple dinosaur to their school. Of course, Henry wasn't about to throw away his first fan mail, even if it smelled like it had been tossed out weeks ago and then salvaged from the trash bins for just this occasion.

Somehow, while he had been in the basement, the rest of the school year had passed and Henry somehow had completed all his exams with excellent scores. Although Henry had defeated Lord Revolting, he had cleverly failed to rescue all the stolen homework. In its absence, the teachers reluctantly admitted that it served no useful purpose, and passed all the students, except Horrendous, of course. The school year was over, and Henry could look forward to a golden summer of abuse followed by more heroism in *Henry Potty and the*

Sequel. His backpack sagged with the weight of magical souvenirs that Henry had borrowed from his unsuspecting teachers.

"Well," he said. "I've completed a whole year here, and understand so much more about the world of gizzardry, not to mention being a California beach bum. Even if I can't bring dear little Goldie back from the dead. So what's in store for me this summer?"

He opened a pamphlet that he'd taken from Bumbling Bore's office when everyone had been too asleep to notice. It read "Straight A students are all invited to come to a day at the happiest place on earth…Wizneyland!" It would be a perfect way to spend his vacation. With any luck, Henry could use his good-deed aura to blind fellow students and sneak to the front of all the lines. He also wanted to spend some time writing his autobiography, a collection of humorous tales about the family car.

Suddenly, Henry was flattened to the ground by a stampede of adoring fans clamoring for autographs and wanting to know when the movie was coming out. Mr. Filth was in the lead, waving a singing and gagging doll that he wanted signed. Perhaps this popularity thing was a bit overdone, was Henry Potty's last conscious thought.

The End

"Wait!"

"What now?" the AUTHOR asked.

"Who gave me that rock at just the right time?"

The AUTHOR sighed. "Henry, you really are a vacuum head. You mailed it to yourself last week, remember? When you did the mysterious, secret errand? It should be totally obvious."

"Oh yeah…"

About the Author

Valerie Estelle Frankel was born at an early age. Since then, she's taught most grades, from kindergarten through high school, and survived with most of her limbs intact. She now teaches creative writing for all ages, and composition for San Jose State University. Her many short stories have appeared in over seventy magazines and anthologies including Legends of the Pendragon, Rosebud Magazine, and The Oklahoma Review. While an undergrad, she became the Editor in Charge of Magical Kingdoms for The Sneeze, a disreputable UC Davis humor publication. She then became the youngest person ever to receive a Master of Fine Arts in Creative Writing from San Jose State University, where she was recently promoted to an office down the hall from the women's bathroom, rather than in it. She enjoys paper napkin collecting, punning, and ridiculous costuming in what little remains of her spare time, and reads a novel every day, just for fun. Many of her short stories lurk on her website, along with writing tips, contests, giveaways, and an interactive fantasy kingdom especially for kids. Readers who long to waste their valuable time can play Chickenfeet Academy Games, check out the Henry Potty eBook, and cavort with flying pigs for hours at www.HarryPotterParody.com.

This and other quality books are available from

OverLookedBooks

Visit us online at:
www.overlookedbooks.com

Printed in the United States
57115LVS00002B/8